Temple Israel Library
Minneapolis, Minn.

Please sign your full name on the above card.

Return books promptly to the Library or Temple Office.

Fines will be charged for overdue books or for damage or loss of same.

OEMCO

Dear Elijah

MIRIAM BAT-AMI

Farrar Straus Giroux

New York

To Sonya and Rachel

ACKNOWLEDGMENTS

I'd like to thank Natalie Spivak, for sharing her stories with me and making excellent suggestions; Rabbi Spivak and Rabbi Cahana, for answering questions; Patricia Kirschner, for her wonderful librarianship; and Esther Hautzig, for taking the time to read this manuscript. Most especially, I'd like to thank Bruce Black, who first believed in the very seed of this story and led me to revisional expansion. And to my editor, Beverly Reingold, thank you so much.

May Elijah sit at all your tables.

Library of Congress Cataloging-in-Publication Data
Bat-Ami, Miriam.
Dear Elijah / Miriam Bat-Ami. — 1st ed.
p.   cm.
[1. Jews—Fiction.   2. Passover—Fiction.   3. Identity—Fiction.
4. Fathers and daughters—Fiction.   5. Elijah (Biblical prophet)—
Fiction.   6. Letters—Fiction.]   I. Title
PZ7.B2939De   1993   [Fic]—dc20   94-29941 CIP AC

When I was a child, I heard so many wonderful stories about biblical heroes. But, of all the heroes, Elijah held a special magical place for me. Unlike Moses, Elijah could actually come into my home. Time was no barrier for him. He lived long ago, but he seemed to keep living.

Elijah, a highly mystical figure, has become one of the most popular heroes in the Jewish tradition. Some see him as an ever-present wise man who wanders around in disguise and aids those in distress. Others associate Elijah with the coming of the Messiah. Elijah is to lead the way. Also, he has a very special role to play during Passover, a springtime holiday that recalls the Israelites' exodus from Egypt and celebrates freedom. Setting the table for the first night's meal, Jews all over the world put out an empty chair for Elijah. In front of his chair, on the table, is his special wine cup, which is filled with wine. During that first meal of Passover, part of the ritual called the Seder, the door is ceremoniously opened for Elijah. He comes in, sips his wine, and departs.

Children and parents often joke about Elijah. How much wine has he drunk? Has any disappeared from the cup? And families all over the world have Elijah stories.

Dear Elijah

March 1

Dear Elijah,

My father is in the hospital. I can't think of anything else to say. I'll write tomorrow.

March 2

Dear Elijah,

In case you didn't check the date, it's tomorrow. I didn't put your address up top because you don't have one. Besides, I'm not going to mail this. I figure that if you are who everyone says you are, Elijah, then I can just leave this in my room and you'll see it. It'll be with the other scrap paper. It'll probably be crum-

3

pled up, too, because I'm not a neat person, and I hate diaries. They are too confining. You have to squeeze everything into little spaces and write on the lines. I like unlined paper that people throw into recycle bins. If I use paper that was going to be thrown away, I don't have to feel that I'm doing something special like writing in MY DIARY with MY SPECIAL PEN. Writing about MY SPECIAL THOUGHTS. I can throw this away any time I want to.

Passover is coming in five weeks, Elijah. What do you do to get ready? Do you move the fiery chariot—you know, the one that took you by a whirlwind into heaven—out of its special parking place in your garage? Does it need an annual chariot checkup and wash? It has to be in good shape to carry you to all those Jewish homes.

Usually by this time we're making plans to clean the house and to order foods. Getting ready is a big job, Elijah. On Passover night you could eat off the rug—that is, if you *did* eat anything and didn't just sip wine.

Mah Nishtanah. Why is this night different from all other nights? I've always liked asking the Four Questions at our Seder. I've liked singing the song that goes with the questions. I've even liked the way we ask the same questions every year and give the same answers. When I was the youngest, I felt extra-special because I got to sing first, since the youngest starts the questions. When you're the smallest child, you almost never get an important job, and you're always last. David, my little brother, must feel that way now. He's only five.

I like that on Passover we eat reclining instead of sitting straight because we're supposed to feel like kings and not slaves. I think of Dad leaning on his big fat pillows on Passover night.

Elijah, why is this year different from all other years?

March 4

Dear Elijah,

It's me again. I'm outside the intensive-care unit. You probably know I'm in the hospital because of the stationery I'm using. I asked a nurse for a piece of paper. She started to give me a new sheet, but I told her I prefer the scraps.

I'm sitting outside because I'm not allowed inside. I don't even know why I'm here, except Mom always wants one of us. Yesterday she brought Sammy, my older brother. We carry kosher food from home on our kosher dishes. My father eats only from kosher plates. When we go on trips, we take our food and plastic dishes with us, but Mom doesn't want Dad using plastic in the hospital. She wants him to feel as if he's at home, because this isn't some fun trip. Dad's not eating yet, but Mom keeps carrying. The nurses must be having a good time with all that chicken and Jell-O.

I wish I could go in. Twelve is an awful age. You're too young to do all the things you want to do, and too old to get out of all the things you don't want to do.

He went in on Saturday, February 27. My father never drives on Saturday, Elijah. It's Shabbes, the day of rest. He never sits in a car and lets himself be driven, either. We're a religious family, Elijah. You must have guessed that when I spoke about the plates. I'm a little bit of a slider, though. Every once in a while I'll break a rule. I started getting into the habit about two years ago. It's hard not to do something wrong every once in a while. But I'm not talking about accidental rule-breaking. This is a conscious kind of thing. I know beforehand what I'm doing, and still I do it. That's why I think I'm sliding. I don't talk about it to the family. I don't talk about how, every so often, I want to do something a little wrong. Nobody would understand. I don't understand myself.

Elijah, don't you think it's hard to do everything perfectly? Besides, I'm not always sure what it means. Does God really care if I eat out of an unkosher plate? And what if my best friend and I go for ice cream and I want to eat out of a dish. Why do I have to get a plastic cup?

Elijah, don't you think God has better things to do than check up on how I'm breaking the rules?

Dear Elijah,

I like my mind to go flabby on the weekend, so I skipped some days of writing. Writing is also forbidden on Shabbes—it's a form of work—and Sundays are for playing. I never do my homework on Sundays. I wake up early Monday mornings and do everything. This morning I woke up super-early and filled in all six math sheets. I even got dressed and had breakfast. I still had an hour to kill, so I read what I wrote you on Thursday. I didn't finish about Dad. It's always very hard for me to stick to the point, Elijah. I never can find that point exactly. Or it seems as if there are so many points.

The ambulance took him to the hospital. He let himself be taken because it was necessary for his health. Dad has broken the Shabbes rules twice: this past Saturday, and twelve years ago when I was born. Dad drove Mom to the hospital. I was born on Friday night. First Mom lit the candles and made a blessing over them so that the spirit of Shabbes, the beautiful Sabbath Queen, could come in. I followed. Dad calls me his Shabbes Princess. I'm not very pretty, though. Only Dad thinks I am.

My father can't see properly, Elijah, even with his twenty-twenty vision. That's why I love him.

March 8—
late Monday night

Dear Elijah,

I can't believe I'm writing you twice in one day. I should try to get some sleep. I hate being tired in school. You have to stretch your eyes wide open to stay awake. I can't sleep, though. My older sister, Fanny, who's in the twin bed next to mine, is snoring so loudly that my mind won't go blank. It keeps counting the time between snores. Then suddenly she stops, and I think fine, I can sleep. Then she starts again.

I can't wait until I have my own room. Fanny is fourteen. In four years maybe she'll go away to college, and I'll have this room all to myself. The wallpaper will need changing first. Fanny chose a white wallpaper with red roses all over it. "Elegant," she says. I get dizzy.

I'm in my bed under the covers, and I have a night-light on. I'm writing you on a piece of lined notebook paper. That doesn't mean this is any more important. I figured that the scraps might get lost, so I found an old three-ring binder that I used in third grade, with my name inside. It's weird. The handwriting is so large. I wonder who that person was who wrote in those large, large letters. I bet she liked writing her name. Right now I'm into long, sharp letters. Especially for my name.

Now I write my name this way, Elijah.

Rebecca

One day I'll write out your name, so you won't forget. You know. When you get old and senile. Do you think forty-six is old, Elijah? That's my dad's age.

Elijah, I must tell you, I'm not much of a writer, even though I have been getting into writing to you. Mainly I enjoy adding on to Mom's grocery lists, especially when she lets me put Breyers SWISS ALMOND FUDGE TWIRL. Some people write about their feelings. I can't do that. I can never figure out what I feel. I'm good at writing *to* people, though, because someone is there who will really read me and maybe answer. I'm not sure why I'm writing to you. I don't expect you to answer. It's just if I wrote all this to one of my pen pals or camp buddies, they'd say, "I'm sorry," and "I hope everything's better." I hate that. I really hate it.

Elijah, what do you do between Passovers? It must take you a whole year to recoup from all that wine. Fanny's really snoring now. *Chah, chah, chaaah.* Two slow ones and then one great powerful one. Are there trade-ins on fiery chariots? How much does the chariot depreciate once it gets off the chariot lot? You might ask me how I know all this. Sammy, who's sixteen, just got his first set of wheels. I like saying "set of wheels." Sammy says that's "stale," which means outdated, but I love old, outdated expressions. I love thinking about "chill out." You'd think the right words would be "thaw out." But maybe when you get cool, then you don't feel anything, and that's good. "Chill out" and "cool it" and "cool as a cucumber" and "cold as ice."

Good night, Elijah. I have to get my beauty rest!

<hr>

March 8—
very late Monday night

Fanny's finally quiet, Elijah, but my mind won't stop making pictures. I've been trying to picture life without a father. My best friend, you know, the one I eat ice cream with, she doesn't have a mother. Her mother died of cancer when she was very small, so she doesn't even remember her mother. When our Girl Scout troop has mother-daughter events, Sheila—that's her name—she goes with her grandmother.

Sheila says that if you don't have a mother and you never had one, you just don't know. But I think she feels bad. I wonder why some kids have, and some don't. And what happens? Afterward. When the heart stops pumping. You know, Elijah, please don't laugh at me, but when I used to fight with my parents, I'd pretend that I died suddenly. I was being buried, and everyone came to the funeral. It was a big affair, Elijah. Everyone was crowded around my casket, and they were crying their eyes out. My parents could hardly stand, they were so grief-stricken, and they felt so guilty. If only they had been nicer to me. But even though I'd be dead, I'd be seeing everything. So I wasn't pretending real death. I never thought about *real* death. Not being. Being gone.

I haven't been doing my homework this week. Nobody cares. Passover without Dad won't be Passover.

March 10

Dear Elijah,

I didn't write yesterday because I was worn out from all that writing. Like I said, I'm used to grocery lists. I am definitely not going to decorate my binder. Some teachers have you decorate your notebook so it's more you. I never know how to decorate. Last year Mrs. Bartlett, our art teacher, had us decorate a box. We were to collect stubs from plays and pictures of things we liked to do. And the box would be us. My box was very sloppy on the outside. Nothing would stick right. And inside, it was empty. Elijah, except for the sloppy part, that is not me. Next time I have a box to do, I'll put a rose inside. And a Hershey's Kiss. And a lemon drop. Then everyone will have to figure out the whole meaning of me. I will be a mystery.

11

Almost two weeks have passed since Dad went in. We are getting used to all of this. You can get used to a lot of things. Mom looks tired, though. Dad can finally eat something, but he'll need surgery. Quadruple bypass. That means all four of the valves to his heart are clogged. Quadruple sounds like so much. After Passover, he's going to a big hospital in Philadelphia for the operation. Then he'll be a new man.

He just has to do things right, Elijah. That's all. He has to keep to a strict diet and get a lot of exercise. That will be hard for Dad. Dad's a baker, and he loves to eat his own food. Sometimes I go with him late at night after Shabbes and make cakes. There's nothing like eating 3:00 a.m. cake batter. You think about how everyone in the whole world is asleep, and you're spooning up cake batter.

Dad'll have to stay away from late-night bakery hours, too. He'll have to leave it all to his assistant.

We are beginning to get ready for Passover. Nobody cares.

Here is your name in fancy script.

Elijah

Keep it for when you're old and senile.

Signed,

The mysterious *moi*

P.S. If you live forever, do you ever get old and senile? In an eternity of living, what's old?

Dear Eliyahu Ha-Navi,

I really shouldn't be writing to you now. Mom lit the Shabbes candles, so I'm not supposed to write. Elijah, lately I've been pretty rebellious. Even before the hospital. Mom says it's a phase. I have to test things. I hate when adults talk about "phases." It makes everything seem so unimportant: "It's a phase she's going through."

One Shabbes I flipped on a light switch in the upstairs hallway. Everyone had to sleep with the light on all night. And I have accidentally on purpose turned on the TV many times. I just sneak up to our third floor, where the TV is. I brush by it, and ZAP it's on. (I don't know why I make it seem as if it's an accident. No one is even there to watch.) Friday night TV is the best. Last Friday I saw *Carrie*. That's a movie about a girl with a wicked mom. Carrie can move things with her mind, and when the pig blood falls on her during the prom, she kills everyone. In the end Carrie gets killed herself, but you're never sure. I'm not going to tell you why not, Elijah. You will have to see the movie yourself. This year I'm going Halloweening as Carrie the Dead Prom Queen.

Elijah, I am beginning to like writing. I am even beginning to think it's okay to write about your feelings, but I will never call this a DIARY. I may, however, keep writing to you, even after Passover. I suppose most people consider you a once-a-year guy. Do you feel neglected the rest of the year? Santa Claus must feel that way, too. Why don't you guys get together and talk about it?

By the way, Santa's last name is Claus. What happened to yours? I had that trouble with my first letter. I wanted to write your full name, and then I realized you don't have one. For this letter I decided to use the Ha-Navi, or "prophet," part for your last name. Don't you have any parents? Maybe if you're a prophet you're just called by your first name, like Amos and Hosea and Ezekiel. Except you're actually called Eliyahu Ha-Navi. Elijah, *the* Prophet. I bet you are Mr. Big Cheese.

I wrote all this, and no one walked into the room. I wonder if I'm even missed. I hate being bugged, and then when no one bugs me, I get annoyed. Why is that so?

Sincerely,

Rebecca Samuelson

(my whole name, in case you haven't guessed)

14

Dear Mr. Big Cheese,

I have been studying up on you. Here is the list of things I know:

You prophesied during the time of Ahab, King of Israel (B.C., not A.D.). Ahab did some no-nos like marrying this very wicked woman named Jezebel and letting her make an altar to Baal, who was the Phoenician god. (If someone calls you a ''Jezebel,'' it means you're a real viper!)

You ran around in a goatskin outfit and warned Ahab that there'd be a drought. Then God told you to hide near a brook. You drank water from the brook. You ate food brought to you by ravens. (What's it like being fed by ravens?)

Later, God commanded you to go back to Ahab, since He was going to stop the drought and send down rain. That's when you decided to have a big contest with the priests of Baal to prove who was worshipping the true God. That must have been some contest. You against four hundred and fifty prophets. Guess who won? (I bet you harty-harred about that one.)

When you left the world, a fiery chariot pulled by flaming horses came down, and you were taken up to heaven in a whirlwind. Elisha, your disciple and Mr. Next-in-Line but never to be Elisha Ha-Navi, was with you.

Elijah, how did you feel when you were with Elisha? I mean, you knew he'd take your place. You yourself anointed him as your successor. God told you to anoint him, so you went to him and threw your mantle on him for a moment. Were you ever jealous of Elisha? When you were showing him the ropes, were you ever afraid? And what is it like to ride a fiery chariot? When Elisha stood on the ground while you ascended, did he see you go up to heaven? Did you go to heaven? And did you miss Elisha? Did you look down and see him, and was that why you finally dropped your mantle for good? I've thought about that, about the words: "Elijah's mantle which had fallen from him . . ." (That's in Kings 2, Chapter 2. I'm sure you know. If *my* life story were written up in the Bible, I'd know the precise words and location.) I figure the mantle didn't fall. You dropped it because it was different from the first time. When you saw Elisha so sad, when you saw him tear his garment in two, you gave your mantle up for good. Nobody commanded you. It was your gift.

I know that Elisha didn't want you to go. You kept telling him to leave you, and he wouldn't. But it was your time, and it happened even while you were together.

Did you want to be alone, going?

What did Elisha feel like when your mantle fell back to earth, and he put it on?

I bet he still missed you. I bet he did.

16

And did you die? If you did, how come you come to us every year?

I know you have many disguises, too, so you won't fool me this year. If I see a beggar, I'll know it's you. If I see a handsome prince, I'll know it's you. If I see a magician, it's you.

The totally black cat was not you. That was really a cat that came through our door three years ago. I'll tell you about it in another letter.

I have been wanting to see you for a long time. I've always wanted to see you because you're magical, and you know. You know how to read people's hearts. You know how to mend hearts that have torn apart.

That's why I began writing. That's the real reason, I guess, besides not wanting to write to a friend. And I didn't want to write to God. Elijah, sometimes I even wonder about God. You know, if there is one. How can we really be sure? There's so much that happens in the world. Yesterday I saw on the news that some guy shot up his wife and his kids, and when the police came he shot himself. Through the head. And then there's AIDS. How do you explain that?

I don't buy into that whole deal of our having limited minds so we cannot comprehend God's plan. I think that's a cop-out. People say that to get out of really thinking.

I have always wanted to talk to you. Always, always. I'm glad I started.

They'll be moving Dad to a private room soon. Maybe I can see him.

Your friend,
Rebecca

P.S. Even if you're a once-a-year guy, I bet you know that your name gets around. Tonight, after Shabbes was over, we sang a song about you. We sing it every Saturday night. Usually Dad leads. Tonight Sammy led. You must know the words, too. About how we hope you come to us in our lifetime. You and the Messiah. We hope, and we wait.

March 14

Dear Elijah,

I think you should know that I like to tell old, stale jokes. Elephant ones are my favorites. I especially like to tell them to Fanny, who hates jokes but always stands there until you're absolutely through and yuk-yukking it up. I always laugh at my jokes. I'm not as bad as Mr. Ginzburg, though. He's a friend of Dad's who comes to our Seder every year and tells the most awful jokes. He even repeats the same ones from year to year. Here are two elephant jokes for you:

1. *How do you know that an elephant has been in the refrigerator?*

2. How do you know that an elephant is in the elevator with you?

Dear Elijah,

Another week of school. Blah. Blah. Generally, I can get into it. I don't usually say that my favorite subjects are recess and lunch. I love reading. Betcha can't guess my favorite all-time book. (Clue: You're not in it!) But right now I can't even seem to concentrate on reading. The words don't stick in my head. I hate rereading the same page over and over again. Another five days. Blah. Blah. Blah.

March 17

Dear E.,

I even got tired of writing to you, but when I woke up this morning, I felt bursting apart with news. I decided to call you E., sometimes. I like saying "E."

19

You couldn't say Dear G. if you were writing to God. E. sounds warm and friendly. Also mysterious.

E., I've told you nearly everything I know about you, but there are things I'm unsure about. As the messenger for the Messiah, will you give out a general announcement? And how will you announce such a thing? Hear ye, hear ye! The Messiah is on his way! The one who will ensure everlasting peace has packed his bags and is due in on the Shabbes shuttle! (In case no one informed you, rumor has it that you will finally arrive with the Messiah in tow some Saturday night.)

Also, how come you were picked to be the Messiah's messenger boy? Is it because you changed? I do think you changed, E., because you started out in the Bible as a very hard person. God even had to show you that He's in the "still small voice," as well as in earthquakes and fire. But then you softened up.

It's funny, Elijah. You weren't the miracle man. Your successor, Elisha, ran around people's homes performing more miracles. Still, I know how you helped this one widow. When you came to her house, her food and oil containers were almost empty, but then they kept filling up. Later you saved her son, who was pronounced dead. You stretched yourself upon the child three times. And God heard you. And the boy revived. You can save children, Elijah. You can save fathers, too. You can turn hearts.

R.

P.S. If I talked to Dad about the way I'm feeling, E., about how I do things accidentally on purpose, he wouldn't be happy. He would turn away. A small part of him would. And there would be nothing you could do.

———

March 18—
after school

Dear E.,

I decided to write outside today. It's so beautiful. I'm sitting in my hideout. We have an hour more until Mom calls us for supper. Fanny and I made this hideout under the pines behind the house several years ago. Fanny never comes here anymore. She makes hideouts for herself without going to secret places. (Some people can do that, E. They can hide out even in public.) We used to have our Readers' Club here. For initiation each member had to swallow a raw egg.

It's only four-thirty, but it's dark under the trees. I'm sitting on pine needles that feel scratchy. The smell is great.

Today I thought I'd write about myself. You don't know much about me except that I like grocery lists and jokes and have two brothers and a sister. There's not much to tell. It's very hard for people to speak about themselves. You know. Objectively.

There are times when I'll look at myself in the mirror and I'll say, "You're okay." Other times I'll look, and a different face looks back at me. A monkey face. The same thing happens with my body. It never stays the same. Actually, I wish it would move along faster. Physically, I'm what you'd call a slow developer. I won't get into that. I doubt you're interested. I am not a looker. I'm so-so. Fanny is the looker in the family. Sammy is the smart one, and David is cute. I'm not sure how the family sees me. I try not to think of that because it's easy to become how you're seen, if you know what I mean. For example, Fanny is the looker, so she feels like she always has to think about her appearance. But she's a lot of other things, too. She's the best modern dancer I know. And she's very smart when she's not trying to be the looker. (I bet you don't want everyone to always see you as the messenger. That's a hard thing to live up to.) I am trying to figure out who I am. I know I like to watch the world around me. People talking, and plants growing and changing. I like to do things, too, with my friends. I have two close close friends: Sheila, the one I told you about, and Linda. I don't like crowds. I like having close friends I can talk to.

Some things I don't tell anyone. I don't like to cry in front of even my best friends. When you cry, you can't think straight. I have to think straight. I also hate talking to Sheila or Linda about Dad. I hate saying words like "heart attack" and "hospital" and "bypass." It makes everything too real. I haven't told anyone about the night it happened, either, and what I saw.

Dad looks very bad. I visited him yesterday—by myself. I snuck in. He was sleeping in a private room. I didn't wake him. I just watched him. When he lies there in that flat bed, he doesn't seem to belong to me. He isn't my father.

I wanted to talk to him, but I was afraid to put stress on his heart. He might have to go back up to intensive care. Things can go any way. He's too weak to travel to Philadelphia for the surgery. We have to wait. Everyone says, "He is a shadow of his former self." Now, what does that mean? Is he really a shadow? Does his former self have a shadow that suddenly walks around instead of the former self?

That's such a stupid phrase. He is very thin, Elijah. When I look at him, I want to cry, but like I said, I don't.

I am not going to write any more about that. It makes me sad, and I don't want to feel. I don't want to feel anything. I will think about you and me. I want to be magical like you and travel all over the world in a second. And never move. I'd love to know things. To look into the face of the Messiah. I've read stories about great rabbis who did that. They went insane. I'd keep my head straight.

What is it like, Elijah, to look into the face of the Messiah? Is it like looking at God? In my mind, God seems so vast and immense. A desert that never ends or one of those trees I saw in California once. I looked up and up, and I still couldn't see the top, so how did I even know it was there?

If I could make God small in my mind, maybe . . . You're different.

March 20

Dear Elijah,
The first day of spring was today. Yay!

Rebecca

March 21

E.,
Two and one half weeks left until Passover. Next year maybe you'll take my notebook with you in the chariot. It'll be your favorite book. You can call it *Dear Elijah* if you like. I never told you my favorite book. That's because it keeps changing.

March 23—
lunchtime

E.,

Do you know that I'm more mad than sad. I'm mad because Dad's not home, and everything is different. We have to do everything without him. I'm mad because he should have taken better care of himself. He should think more about himself and less about us. I'm mad because sometimes it feels good to have him away. It really does, Elijah. You don't have to always be thinking of rules. Mom's religious, but she bends a little. She doesn't get all hyped up if something just a little unkosher slips into the house. You have to be perfect around him all the time. It is very hard being perfect. When Dad's home, Elijah, the house feels full of the spirit of Judaism. When he's gone . . . but he's a very hard person. He thinks he's right. And he never tells you how he really feels. When he gets mad, he gets quiet. I hate quiet anger.

R.

Date: March 23—evening
To: Eliyahu Ha-Navi (E.H.)
From: Rebecca Samuelson (R.S.)
Re: The Passage of Time

How do you like that, Elijah? I just learned memo writing and thought I'd practice so I wouldn't forget. Maybe I should get a fax number. Are you up on modern machinery, Elijah? A fax is a machine that'll zap a letter from one place to another in a minute. Maybe one day we'll be able to fax across time. Then I can send some hot message to Moses like: "Have someone watch your people. They're about to make a false God."

In case you don't know, Elijah, there are only two more weeks left to Passover. That's fourteen days.

Passover. Pesach. Festival of Spring. I want to think spring thoughts, but I seem stuck in winter. When Dad comes home . . .

I'm tired of talking about me and Dad and how nothing's getting done here.

Goodbye!

Dear Elijah,

I don't think you really exist. You're like Santa Claus. Or the tooth fairy. Or the Easter bunny. Or what's-His-name, you know, old G–O–D. SOMEBODY MADE YOU UP BECAUSE THEY WERE SCARED!

March 25

E.,

I don't like being scared. I don't like not knowing. I am a person who eats a toasted bagel every morning because it makes me feel good. I eat a toasted bagel, and butter, and cherry jelly with real cherry pieces in it. Mom has tried to get me to eat cereal and eggs, but I like the bagel. I like to know that I'll wake up and I'll walk into the kitchen and the bagel will be there.

It makes me feel good.

I don't like being scared at all.

Dear E.,

You know, sometimes I feel like you're inside of me, which is funny because you're not really inside. Maybe it's because when I'm writing you I'm thinking about you, but I'm talking to myself. I know the writing stays in my mind, too, even though I don't go back and check.

E., anything can happen. Anything. Don't you feel that way? I bet you do. I bet sometimes you think that if you close your eyes, the Messiah will come. Or the world will end.

For at least a year I've felt that way. I cry for no reason. Absolutely none. And normal things seem different. When we had our first snowfall in the winter, I felt as if I had never seen snow before. I ran outside and threw scoopfuls of snow into the air. Like a kid. Except I'm almost a teenager. And when the birds came back from wherever they go in the winter, suddenly, one day last week, I heard them. I was standing at the kitchen window, and their singing went straight into my heart. I wanted to cry, too, because I thought of how it had been so silent all January and February and clear into this month, except I hadn't noticed. And then there was so much sound. My whole chest wanted to burst apart.

Elijah, there are times when I'm walking, and I feel

heavy as a huge rock. I can hardly move myself from one place to another. Then, poof, I'm as light as a feather. I put my feet down on the cement, and I can't feel the ground. I am that light.

And all year long I've been feeling . . . I can't breathe because my chest is so full. It's full with the sound of things I can't even name. Nameless, invisible things.

Sometimes I want to laugh all day long. Sometimes I hate everybody. Especially phonies. I hate phonies most of all. In case you didn't know, Mr. Big Cheese Eliyahu Ha-Navi, this whole world is full of fakes. The synagogue is jam-packed with them. People who bug the living daylights out of me. I'd like to pop them, E. I'll sit in the synagogue and I'll watch Mrs. Levine walk in with her hat, and Mrs. Cohen, who looks like a horse, will be making some comment. Right during the time when someone is chanting a passage from the Holy Bible, and you are supposed to be quiet! And when he prays, Mr. Jacobs screams at the top of his lungs so everybody can hear that he knows all the words. Sometimes Mr. Weinfeld will have a contest with Mr. Jacobs. One will try to out-shout the other. And when you have to stand and pray silently to yourself, Weinfeld and Jacobs bounce up and down like regular pogo sticks. It makes me sick. So I stare at the ceiling.

I think about God. I close my eyes and wonder. How do I know? How do I really know? So I say to myself, "If I get a sign by five o'clock this evening, then the fix is in." The sign doesn't come. Still, Elijah, I'll look at the smallest thing: I'll see a bee shoving his face into the lavender we have at the side of our house, or I'll touch one of my squash blossoms . . . I make my own garden in the summer, E., next to Mom's. I love the way squash blossoms open. They're as thin as paper. And yellow. And wrinkly soft. And when the sun beats down on them, they fold up.

I love to walk on the grass early in the morning when it's still wet and cold.

I love to walk in my bare feet and feel the grass between my toes. And once I saw baby finches hatching. There were six eggs in the impatiens plant Mom hung on our porch, and I saw them. I saw the mother nesting on them. And my heart burst apart then.

I must have a very strong heart, the way it keeps bursting.

Everything seems so miraculous. It all has meaning. And when I'm in synagogue with all these people, when we're all praying, saying the words together, E., sometimes I'll look at the hat wearers and pogo sticks, and I'll see this other thing, too. As if God came down or we were brought up. Scooped up.

Or it's a Jewish holiday like Succoth, the thanksgiving festival. All my family is sitting out in a booth made of wood and decorated with gourds and fruit and birds that we all made, birds with paper tails

30

. . . Did you ever eat your dinner inside a little hut in your yard, E.? Did you ever stare up through the pine-branch ceiling to see the stars?

I can't explain, E. Lately I've been mad because I just want to be me. I want to be like everybody else, too. I want to see a movie on Saturday. I want to shop at the mall with my friends who aren't so religious and stop for pizza that's not strictly kosher. I even want to have a tree with lights. And presents. Not exactly a Christmas tree. I don't know.

I want to be Jewish, Elijah. I am Jewish. But what would happen if I stopped being very religious? And what is religious? Does it mean following all the rules? What are the right rules? You know, there are people *more* religious than our family. And there are people who don't follow any particular rules at all, and they feel religious. I have a friend like that. Her family watches a church show on TV. They don't go to a regular church, but sometimes my friend's dad will get into talking about how he sees nature and how it makes him feel spiritual. What is spiritual, Elijah?

I am deep-down Jewish, Elijah. But I don't want Dad being there all the time, making me remember. No one has to tell me how to think and feel. How to be! Because when I am in synagogue or staring up at the stars . . .

I can be a very spiritual person, Elijah.

Dear Mr. Messianic Messenger,

How come Sammy saw you and I didn't? I don't think that's fair, particularly because ever since I was little I have been waiting for you. Not every day. Just around Passover. I've been hoping. And praying. But Sammy saw you first.

Last year, late at night, when we were all sleeping, Sammy said that he snuck downstairs. "I saw him," he said. "I saw the old man. He was sipping wine from his own special wine cup and smacking his lips." (Sammy called you "the old man," not me.)

"He was pleased," said Sammy. "Elijah loves Manischewitz Concord Grape wine."

"How do you know he was Elijah?" I asked. "Maybe he was a thirsty burglar."

"He was Elijah."

"Did he tell you so? Did he tell you he has a preference for Concord Grape over Cherry? And then did he say, 'By the way, my name is Elijah. Elijah, the prophet, messenger of the Messiah. Pleased to meet you.' "

"You mean, did Elijah and I have a conversation the way humans have conversations? No, silly. Elijah isn't someone you have a chat with."

Fanny and I thought that Sammy snuck downstairs

and drank the wine himself. But how could you argue if you haven't seen Elijah yourself.

AND YOU NEVER SHOWED YOURSELF TO ME, MR. ELI-JAH! I THINK I DESERVE TO SEE YOU, PARTICULARLY SINCE I'M THE ONE WHO OPENS THE DOOR.

Every year it has been my special job to open the door for you. It's one of my favorite parts of the Seder. I am not saying it's such a big deal! But I happen to like the opening. I get to thinking how everyone is waiting for me. Even my father is waiting.

"Rebecca," Dad says.

I pull back my chair. I don't look at anyone. I look toward the doorway. Then I walk slowly through the long Sinai desert that extends from our living room to the front entrance of our home. I know Sammy is snickering. I can feel his snicker bore into my back. But I still walk slowly. I want to make the walk last forever.

Sometimes, Elijah, I can feel you inside of me or across from me or speaking out across eternities of sand, but I've never seen you. Not in the flesh and blood. Sammy thinks you look like an old man. I think you can look like anything you want. When I write, sometimes you look a little like my dad, but you're not him. You're someone I can talk to. Sometimes I imagine you very young. You look like Barry Cohen, who's this boy in my class. I have always wanted to touch the back of his neck. I am a sucker for boys' necks.

E., you look positively wonderful. And you're riding your chariot.

You invite me for a ride. Inside the fiery chariot. (It had a tune-up, by the way. It has also been painted.)

You hold out your hand.

And I walk through fire.

Love,

R.

Some extra thoughts: I wonder if you are things even you don't know about. You're trying to figure yourself out. You've been doing that all your eternal life. You keep changing. But we keep seeing you in the same way. We keep using the same labels, the way the family does with Fanny, the "looker," and Sammy, the "smart one." I like to think of you changing, E. Of my not knowing. Sometimes I even wish I could wait for you forever. Oh, E., it seems like I've been waiting forever for so many things. Like "it," which is what girls say when they're talking about "it" and how it's about time "it" came already. I want "it" badly, but once it comes it will be part of my life. Just another thing. Now it's something to wait for. Waiting can be good and bad. I hate waiting for Dad to get better. I hate not knowing about him.

E., I am going to wear a spring skirt to school tomorrow. It'll swish around my legs. I'll wear my pink blouse that's not a feminine pink. It's shocking pink. Cold pink. I love it!

R. (again)

March 28—
Sunday morning

Dear E.,

I know you're not God. And writing to you isn't praying. When I was little, I used to talk to God all the time. I'd say my prayers, and then I'd say how God should bless all the family. Then I'd talk to God. About my friends. And fights with my sister. I'm always fighting with Fanny. But these past couple of years I haven't talked to God. He seems so far away. Like someone I pray to in synagogue. Somebody who couldn't be bothered.

You're different.

R.

Same evening
(not doing homework
but writing to you)

Dear Elijah,

I looked over everything I wrote to you, and I didn't think that I was a total jerk. I even made corrections and recopied sloppy work. I wanted to see it neat.

I saw that I never gave you the answers to my elephant jokes. Have you guessed yet? I also never finished the story about the black cat. I am going to tell you it now.

All of this happened three years ago, when I really thought I was going to see you. I was standing with my back against the open door. I was just about to say, "Welcome, Elijah," when suddenly a black cat appeared out of nowhere. I was looking into the dark street, and this thing separated itself from the rest of the blackness.

It was as if the cat had been waiting for me, E. I stood glued to the door. The black thing darted straight through the living room to the dining area. Then it ran around the Seder table once, gobbled up a piece of chicken that had fallen under my seat, and ran out. I couldn't tell where it had run off to. It just melted into the blackness again.

It happened so fast that no one said anything—not at first. Then my little brother, David, who was real little then—only two—he broke the silence. "Tat," he shouted, giggling and pointing to the door that I hadn't closed. I was still glued to the screen.

"Tat!" David repeated.

Everyone laughed. We all knew the cat was only a cat, but we needed someone to tell us. Somebody small like David. I laughed, too, E. But I really wanted to cry. I kept thinking how I'd have to wait a year before I'd see you. *Maybe* see you. I'd have to go through a host of other Jewish holidays before Passover rolled around again.

I unglued myself from the screen and walked slowly back to my seat.

"Better luck next time," said Sammy, winking.

"You know," said Fanny in her real dramatic voice, "yesterday I saw God. He came to me in a dream."

E., a long line of famous people have come to Fanny in her dreams, and they're always doing things for her. She doesn't dream about classmates, the way I do. She dreams about Moses, and Cleopatra, Queen of the Nile, and Clark Gable, and Tom Cruise. Cleo tells Fanny that her beauty is divine. Moses says that she is the most spiritual thing he has ever laid eyes on. Gable says that he's been tossing in his grave, thinking about Fanny. Cruise takes a picture of her to every movie set he works on.

"In another life I was a very famous person," says Fanny.

The family is in Fanny's dreams, too, but we're always slaves. We're constantly bowing down to her. Just last week Fanny said how she was Joseph in her dreams. Sammy and I were Joseph's bad brothers. (Sammy and I are always the bad ones in Fanny's dreams.) Fanny-Joseph was the moon or the sun, she can't remember which, and we were bowing down to her.

"You remember how all the sheaves bowed down

to Joseph and that meant he'd be ruler, and his brothers would have to obey him," said Fanny, frowning at Sammy and me. "Well, in my dream, you guys were the sheaves of wheat, bending down before me. I was looking down on you and wondering if I should show mercy."

Fanny's unconscious mind is just consumed by dreams of power. That's why when Fanny began on God three years ago, nobody was surprised. "He came to me inside a white pillar of fire," said Fanny. "He told me that I should be patient. I shouldn't scream at Sammy and Rebecca even if they're idiots. They simply don't have as high a consciousness as I do."

E., I have never really wanted to have dreams like Fanny's. I have never really cared about seeing God or Moses, either. I've never needed to see them. I've just always wanted to see you.

"Elijah," I will say, "sit down a spell. Rest your weary feet."

And then I will look down. At your feet. How worn they must be.

You'll say, "My chariot is waiting."

The horses will be neighing and pawing. Flame will come out of their throats and their eyes. Their manes will be red with flames.

I'll walk through fire, and then I'll touch your hand.

And questions will be answered. And I'll know.

E.,

I'm thinking about Passover. Dad will be home. I hope he will be. The doctors aren't sure yet. And Passover will be the way it always was. We'll do everything we always do. The frenzied preparation. The Seder.

While we march through the Seder, you will wait outside, just as the black cat waited. And when I open the door, saying, "Welcome, Elijah!" you will come in. Invisibly. You will sit on a seat reserved especially for you, where your tall wine cup stands, full to the brim, and when you sip, nobody will see it—except me. Your wine cup will stay full, but I'll see you drinking. I will not be seeing you with my normal eyes. I will see you with my spirit eyes. You will see me with your spirit eyes, too, the ones you use all the time.

I will not let on, E. The miracle will sit inside my soul even while I see your lips turn purple with wine, and when I look at you, I'll hear you talking, even while your lips are still. You and I do not need lips to talk.

"It'll be fine," you'll say. "Don't worry."

When we are all done singing, when David's on the

39

floor fast asleep and I'm yawning, you'll leave. I won't even see you leaving because if I saw you, I'd say, "Stay. Please stay." My eyelids will shut, just for a second, and you will leave as you came. Invisibly.

I do not know how I'll feel. Maybe I will want to pray. Maybe I won't.

March 29—
eight more days left
until Passover

E.,

This morning, before school, I went to the hospital. Dad woke up. He asked about holiday preparations. We're way behind. Mom told him that everything's going on schedule, but it's not. I took Dad's breakfast. Sammy and Fanny have been relieving Mom because she has been bringing Dad his meals three times a day for a month now. I finally convinced her to let me help out, too.

When you go into a hospital, it's like you're entering into another world. It has its own language. Every place has a language, I guess. Even school has its own language. Every place has its own smells, too. Hospitals smell like medicine and waxed floors.

In the outside world, there are so many differences. Outside, people are rich or poor or from the East or from the West, or they're starting out in life or getting ready to retire. Outside, you don't have a mother or you do. You're black or white. You're Jewish or Christian. You're a boy or you're a girl. And everybody keeps reminding you of differences.

But in a hospital you're either a patient or a visitor—or someone who takes care of patients or visitors. This morning I was the visitor. Dad was the patient. I didn't like it.

E., it seems like I'm always scared now. I go to bed scared. And I get up scared. Eating bagels for breakfast doesn't help, either. And I haven't started to pray because I can't figure out the words I need, and I'm still not sure about God. He's there somewhere. I just don't know where to look.

Anyway, when I went inside Dad's room, I felt strange because he still doesn't look like my dad. I mean, I know he's Dad, but I keep thinking that he must be someone else's father. Someone who has a thin father. So I didn't know what to do.

The food felt heavy in my hands because I was just standing there, looking, which didn't bother him, since he was sleeping when I walked in. His prayer book was on his chest. The man who is my father, Elijah, has such a thin chest. I could see it underneath his pj's. They were green pj's that Mom bought him last week. Mom bought Dad a new robe and pj's. Fanny and Sammy chipped in together for a great new pair of slippers. I haven't figured out what to get Dad

41

yet. I keep looking around. I can't find the right present. I told David I'd add his name to my gift because he only has a penny jar filled. Now David keeps bugging me about when I'm going to get *our* present.

I didn't look too much at Dad's chest. It's not right to stare at your father's chest, especially when it doesn't look like your father's chest. I put the food on the table near his bed and sat down. I kept clasping and unclasping my hands. My fingernails are very gross because I've started biting them, and they're jagged. I don't care. Then I got to thinking what it would be like if I were on the bed sleeping, and he were watching. And it were me instead of him.

I know he'd pray, Elijah. He'd pray, and his prayers would rise all the way up. Clear up to heaven. Because the fix is in between my father and God. My father knows the route his prayers are supposed to take. But everybody's route is different. Don't you know? Everybody has a different route.

Later

When I was writing to you, Elijah, my mind shut off. I was thinking how I got mad watching Dad, and then my mind shut off. Just like that. I guess I was feeling how mad I had been in the hospital.

MY FATHER IS SUPPOSED TO PROTECT ME, E. HE IS NOT SUPPOSED TO BE SICK. HE IS SUPPOSED TO LIVE FOREVER AND EVER AND BE MY DAD!

I was clasping and unclasping my hands. Being quiet as a mouse. Looking at Dad's prayer bag, which was next to his chest. Ever since Dad came into the hospital, he's kept his prayer book and the tallis bag with his prayer shawl in it right up close to him. When he was in intensive care, he asked Mom to bring him the prayer bag. Maybe he was thinking about the right thing even then. He'd die, and we'd have to put him into a plain coffin. We'd have to make sure he was buried in his prayer shawl. Maybe he thought we wouldn't find it.

Or maybe he just needed it around him. My father has the most beautiful prayer shawl. And he believes. In God. In Judaism. In the rules. He believes with a kind of perfect belief. Everything about me is imperfect. I don't know what I want. I want to be a girl, and I am, but I also want to start being a woman. Sheila already is, you know, in a physical way. And sometimes I want to be the me that's not a girl—you know, just a kid. Sometimes I wonder what it would be like if I were totally different. I'd like to be a boy for a while, just a while. I'd like to be black, too. I'd like to feel it from the inside. And I'd like to be someone whose native language isn't English. I'd like to speak English with a foreign accent. Everybody would try to guess where I'm from. I wouldn't let on.

43

Elijah, so often lately I've felt trapped in a cage. I want to burst out. I want to dive underwater. I want to kiss a boy underwater. I'd hold my breath forever.

So I start doing funny things. I don't tell the family that. I don't even tell my dad. Lately I've been telling you, even though I'm not sure about you. Not at all. Maybe all of this is to me. It doesn't matter. I just want to write about what I feel because when I write, I can hold on. I can look at things, and I don't feel so confused, though I'm still afraid.

I felt like I was sitting next to Dad forever. I kept clearing my throat because I wanted him to get up already, but I didn't want him to think I woke him on purpose. When Fanny snores and keeps me up, I do that: I clear my throat loudly and sigh, "Oh, oh!" Then she turns over on her side and stops snoring.

I cannot wait to have my own room. My own private room.

I stood watching my dad and clearing my throat. Mainly I was staring at his toes. I am not used to seeing my father's toes. Except when he's swimming. Otherwise he pads around in his socks or in the slippers that he wears in the bakery. (I should have gotten Dad the slippers!) "Your father has ugly toes," my mother says.

I have to admit that they are ugly. Especially the toenails.

Then I started setting the hospital table. I made a small racket with the dishes, and he woke. We started talking the way we always do. Dad was saying the same old things. It's like a ritual. Like the Four Questions. The same questions. The same answers. Except nothing is the same this year.

"The Shabbes Queen," Dad said, smiling at me.

"She came and went already," I said. "It's Monday."

"I didn't get a chance to say it on Friday."

"It doesn't matter. I'm not the Queen, anyway."

"Then who are you?"

"The Princess."

I didn't want to say "The Princess," E. I don't know what I wanted to say. Maybe the Decorator of Boxes. The Future Writer. The Thief or the Liar. The Girl Who Is in Love with Spring. The Chariot Rider. But I said "The Princess" because right now Dad needs to know that the whole world outside is going along just as it always has. Nothing has changed, even when we all know everything has changed. Besides, I don't want to fight. Not now.

Maybe one day, Elijah, I'll walk into his room, and I'll be ready. Or maybe I'll just walk out the door. It'll be time for me to move out on my own. And then it'll be my house. And my rules. Except I'll have children, too.

I'm still a young person, Elijah. I can't stretch my mind that far ahead. But I don't want to fight.

Dad smiled.

"You look good," I said, touching my lips to his

cheek. It felt so fine and thin, like paper that would tear any minute.

"I look terrible, and you are a very bad liar. Everything shows in your face."

I blushed because I knew it was true: I can't lie very well. When I don't want to tell the truth, I just hide out. Soon enough, everyone forgets. The world is a very busy place.

"You should eat," I said.

"You sound like your mother."

"Is that bad?"

"No. How are the Pesach preparations going? Has your mother ordered all the food? Are you all cleaning up?"

For a second I wanted to say that all our food would be *chometzdik*, all leavened, all forbidden. I wanted to say that we had ordered fifty boxes of spaghetti for the two ritual meals. But I didn't. "Everything's fine," I said, looking away so he wouldn't read my face. "Eat."

I sat on the bed next to Dad. We ate together. Dad hates to eat alone. He hates to *be* alone, too. He's scared of the dark, which is odd when you think about how he works at night. He keeps all the bakery lights on and works. It's funny: he's a man with such perfect faith, and he has so many friends, and until all of this happened he never seemed scared of anything—except the dark.

I like the dark. I like imagining that I'm a night-time creature. All the human world is asleep. Eyes are closed everywhere. And I'm up.

I ate a slice of toast and marmalade. Dad and I both love orange marmalade. Dad had toast and cereal. Everything was cold.

"I miss Shabbes at home," he said, fingering his prayer bag. "Mondays are all right, but Shabbes in a hospital is no Shabbes."

"We did everything we were supposed to do," I said. I don't know why I said that. My father wanted me to say how much we missed him. How much the house is falling apart without him. He wanted me to tell him that everything is on schedule, but we're all messed up. Because he is Mr. Big Cheese. Without him everything should be a mess. But my heart felt very hard.

"Everything is in order," I said. "We'll be ready."

Then he looked at me. My father has large eyes. Sometimes they look brown. Sometimes they look green. They're the one thing about him that's not definite. "I married him for his eyes," says Mom.

They seemed so large inside his face. Inside his thin face.

I don't like seeing my father so thin. It's like a part of him is missing. You see it in your mind, but you don't see it when you look. It's very, very confusing. I don't like seeing his thin chest and his ugly toes. I don't like watching him fingering his prayer bag. I don't like eating his cold toast and making up lies

47

about Passover. I don't like to think about how I want to hurt him even though I love him.

My father is not perfect, E. I could see that. When he looked at me, I could see so much. How he can't bear the thought of not being missed. How he hates to think of life going on without him. And he's scared. Even with his direct route and his tallis bag and the fix that's in, he's very afraid. Because you can never be sure of what happens. When you stop breathing. Not totally, totally sure.

"We miss you at home," I said. Then I walked out.

⸻⸻

March 30—
seven more days
until Passover

Dear Elijah,

In case you're wondering why my binder looks different and where some of the stains came from, this is how it happened. When I got home from the hospital, I almost threw the binder in the trash. I felt so tired. I took out all these sheets. You'd be surprised, Elijah, at how much I've written. I put all my sheets in the can. I threw them in. Then I stood over the trash. I stood a long time. I didn't like to see all my paper with the other trash. I didn't like to think of it getting dirty and being thrown out. What if you

48

came, and you opened my binder, and you found nothing? What if you've been reading all along? What if you even have eye strain from all that reading? *Hah!*

I picked up all the sheets. I don't think I did it for you, E. A few sheets are a little stained. But there's nothing gross on them. Then I started to decorate my binder. It's prettier that way.

Still seven more days

Dear Chariot Rider,

I forgot to tell you that we are finally, finally getting ready. Maybe we'll even be ready for you. We are being very crazy here. Bob Ginzburg ordered some boxes of special *shmura matzo* for us. (If you've forgotten, E., Bob G. is the one who tells the awful jokes.) Every Passover we order a few boxes of handmade *shmura matzo* from Israel. It tastes like hard burnt crackers, but I love it. This year we totally forgot. B.G. took care of it.

Mom woke up this morning. She ran down to the hospital. She complained about the nurses and the staff and the food and the doctors—which made her feel real good—and then she said, "Pesach. It's time!"

Then Mom and I sat at the kitchen table together.

Mom was finally making her famous Passover list. "Number one," she said, "soup." Mom wrote it down.

"Number one," I whispered, "chocolate-covered matzos." I liked being there with her. I liked the way it just felt usual. Like every year.

"Number two," said Mom, more loudly, "kosher-for-Pesach wine."

"Number two," I said, "Passover brownies."

Both of us tapped our pencils.

"Cherry jelly," muttered Mom in a maniacal way. "Kosher-for-Pesach toothpaste! Soap!"

Mom wrote furiously. I stared at the daisies on our kitchen wall, upside-down daisies that almost never touch each other.

"Brownies!" I shouted back. "Sponge cake! Hershey's Kisses!"

My pencil point broke. On the wall the daisies bumped into each other, falling.

And, oh, E., I could taste all those Passover delights in my mouth: cakes that come in aluminum cake pans, funny Passover cakes that aren't made with flour. *Matzo brei*, made with eggs and matzos that Mom and I soften by putting them into boiled water. *Matzo brei* covered with jelly. Butter-and-jelly sandwiches on matzo. Cheese and lettuce sandwiches on matzo. Macaroons. Chocolate macaroons! Coconut macaroons! Millions of macaroon mounds stretching across the whole Sinai desert.

E., I wanted Passover to come already.

March 31—
six more days!

Dear E.,

Mom and I went down to Benji's today, E. Benji's is the one Jewish delicatessen in our town, where we can all eat a meal. Usually we go to Benji's once or twice a month, but before Passover Mom rushes down there at least once a day. Each time she goes she takes one of us kids.

Mom's muttering had reached a fever pitch. Occasionally I'd catch a word or two like "Shabbes candles" or "flanken." I bet you like boiled beef flank, E. I bet you're even partial to houses where flanken is being served. "Rest your weary feet, Elijah. Have some boiled beef." Maybe that's why it has taken the Messiah so long to come. As he approaches, he gets a whiff of the Messianic meal—B.B. with stewed prunes on the side—and he retreats for another decade or so. If you haven't guessed, Elijah, flanken is on my never-touch-it list. So is tongue. Tongue is on my never-touch-it, never-look-at-it list. How can anyone in his right mind eat tongue? Maybe the Messiah prepared himself for the entry twice already. Once he smelled B.B., and he backed off. No doubt that disappointed you. You were all ready for the Hear-ye, Hear-ye announcement. On the Messiah's second venture out, someone had a platter of tongue waiting for him. Who knows what will coax him out now. I'm not sure even my mother's wonderful matzo balls will work.

Mom entered the kosher deli armed with slips of paper: kosher liquid detergent, kosher-for-Pesach wine, egg matzos, plain matzos. The slips spilled out of her coat. I slid in behind her.

Benji was standing at the counter behind the meat slicer. Elijah, Benji is big and fat, probably because he samples all his food. And sometimes I think that he and his meat slicer are one being. When Benji inserts meat into the slicer and peels off roast beef slices, his hand continues the slicer action. It's always under the slicer when the meat falls. And it always moves from the slicer to the waiting wax paper at the same speed.

Benji deftly wrapped up a package of sliced turkey. He wiped his hands on his white apron. "A little late this year," he said, grinning at Mom.

"I've been busy."

I could tell Benji was trying to figure out how he was going to raise the "touchy" issue. Say it already, I kept thinking.

"How's the husband?" Benji finally asked. On the mend, I said silently in my mind.

"On the mend," said Mom.

That's what Mom tells everyone, E. I wonder if she believes it.

"Give him my best," said Benji. "And tell him I'll stop by and visit. Maybe, too, I should bring him the corned beef he likes so much."

Mom frowned. "No more corned beef. Too fatty."

Benji looked sad. You could tell he hated thinking about life without corned beef. "Will he be home for the holidays?"

"We hope so."

"Give him my best."

I stood next to Mom, thinking that the conversation was going nowhere. If we stood there much longer, Benji would be asking about Dad's room and the service and just how the heart attack happened. And Mom has said it a hundred times. How he fell. Where he landed. How much blood.

Then, after all the gore, he'd say again, "Give him my best."

I pushed Mom forward. She seemed to be frozen in one place. That happens, too, E. A person asks my mother about Dad, and she freezes. Then, even if no one asks her, she says it: How he fell. Where he landed. How much blood. How she called. The way she felt.

Mom unfroze herself. She took in the store. She was her old self, at least for a second. She was assessing the layout. She knew if Benji had good meat. She had spied it out. She had also spied out the stale sesame seed candies.

Benji grinned at me and shifted the yarmulkah that he keeps on his head with a black bobby pin. No doubt, I thought, Benji will slip the Messiah a few stale sesame seed candies. He will be preparing a Messianic sack lunch, and the cellophane-wrapped

sesame seed candies will be hidden under the bagel-
and-lox-and-cream-cheese sandwich. The lox will be
the salty kind, too. Still, there will be something in
that sack lunch so good that the Messiah will forgive
Benji. It'll be green, and sour-tasting, and juicy, and
it will come from Benji's famous barrel.

"You want a pickle, Rebeccaleh?" Benji asked,
seeming to read my mind. Together we positioned
ourselves over the large pickle barrel. Fat warty shadows swam around silently like green sharks inside a
sea of salt and brine. My mouth watered.

"This one," said Benji, poking a large fork into the
vat and dragging up a huge green wrinkled thing.
"This one is the largest."

Juice dripped from the captured pickle. Benji
wrapped it in wax paper and presented it to me.
"Maybe your dad would like one?" he whispered.

"No pickles!" shouted Mom. (Elijah, my mother
has amazing ears. She can hear through walls. She
also smells from miles away. It's uncanny.)

I wanted to tell Benji to save one of those juicy
pickles for the Messiah, but I didn't. I know, though,
that when it is time for the Messiah to recount his
best meal, he will talk of Benji's pickles. He will
forget the boiled beef and the tongue and the stale
sesame seed candies. He'll be so amazed by the pickles. And Benji will have a new sign in front of his deli:
"The Messiah ate here."

Mom walked through the store, pointing here,

54

pointing there. Benji raced behind her. His flat black shoes, which are always covered with a thin layer of dust, made quiet ballet-slipper sounds. Boxes descended.

"Don't forget the sponge cake," I whispered to Mom. "And the bubble gum."

Benji opened a square cardboard box filled with gold tinfoil coins that came all the way from Israel. Inside the foil was pink bubble gum sprinkled with powder. I watched Benji, and I thought about how Israeli kosher-for-Passover gum isn't sweet like American bubble gum. It isn't soft, either. It doesn't even make bubbles. It's hard to chew, and it can take your fillings out. One year it even tore apart Sammy's braces. He had to spend an entire day with wire poking into his cheek. But we all love that gum. And you can't explain it. Maybe it's the gold foil that makes it look attractive. Or maybe it's because it comes from Israel, that faraway place where so many Jews live. I'm in the United States. I'm chewing hard, powdery gum. And in Israel, across the entire globe, tons of other children are doing that, too. We are all remembering the Exodus from Egypt.

Benji handed me a paper bag, and I dropped the gold Israeli gum coins inside. And, oh, E., my heart felt bursting again. I love Passover. I love the way it comes every year. I love the sameness of it. I love how our house becomes a different house. Not a regular *chometzdikeh* house, Elijah. An altogether different house.

Then we were back at the counter, Benji and Mom and me.

"I don't want any of last year's leftovers," said Mom, towering over the candies on display. "Fresh! We need fresh!"

Benji winked at me and returned a tin of yellow and red and green sour balls to its old hiding place. I crunched on my pickle. No one fools Mom, I thought.

April 1, 1:30 p.m.—
five more days!

Dear E.,

Late at night, I imagine Dad's heart. It is sitting on a long white table, and it is huge and red and pumping furiously. Around it are angels. I know they're angels. They have their angel wings on. And they are sewing Dad's heart.

In and out. In and out.

They sew with red thread so you can't see the stitches. And while they sew, their wings fan Dad's heart.

In and out. In and out the threads move. The wings fan. And the angels hum softly to themselves, "On the mend. On the mend."

And when they are done, when they are all done

stitching Dad's heart together, everything seems perfect. Except now there are seams.

"What you have to do," says Mom, "is let him know that you're here for him. We're all here for him."

April 1—
2:15 p.m.

Dear Elijah,

The Messiah came without you. You were taking one of those year-long naps, and the Messiah slipped through the gates of heaven to earth. Better luck next time on performing your duty as messenger.

Sincerely,
Rebecca

April 1—
2:50 p.m.

Dear E.,

Did I fool you? It's April Fools'. I thought I'd try a Messiah trick on you. Yes, I'm in class. Bulldog (the nickname we gave our teacher because her face is pugged and she has weensy bulldog eyes) is going on and on about some general during the American Revolution. She started her big lecture about 1:00! Some classes get to do battle reenactments. Kids get to wear eighteenth-century clothes. Not us. We just memorize. I hate learning that way. I thought I'd write you instead of taking notes. Besides, everybody expects me to be a poor performer these days. I might as well play it for all it's worth.

E., what do you think about the afterlife? Somehow it's hard for me to imagine that there are separate heavens, like one for Jews and one for non-Jews, or one for people and one for animals. I think that if you're good, then you deserve a good afterlife. No matter who you are. And if you're just following animal instinct, then you should go to heaven, too, even if you're a ferocious lion.

What do you think, Mr. Eternity Traveler?

And how do you feel about being Jewish? When I do all these Passover rituals, I don't feel alone. I think about all those people in Israel, and in countries all over the world, who are preparing for Passover. I think back to all the Jews who have readied themselves. I am part of some ancient ritual that goes on and on. An unchanging ritual.

It feels good to be part of something that never changes. It feels good to imagine some changes. When I grow up and live in my own house, when I have a husband and children, we'll tell the story of

Passover. We'll observe the rules and remember to tell. We'll read the *Haggadah*, which is the telling story. But our voices will be our voices. When we explain, we'll have our own explanations.

Maybe the first night of Passover, my family will sit at Mom and Dad's table. We'll follow their story.

The second night, we'll all sit at our table.

You'll be with all of us, Elijah. You'll be thinking about how you saved the boy. How you looked down on my father, too.

I am asking you to help my father, E.

Friday, April 2—
four days
and still counting

Dear E.,

Do prophets get strep? I'm home with strep. It is highly contagious. What if we all come down with it and really have to cancel the holiday celebration entirely? Mom is frantic. She does not need any more sick people. This morning I couldn't swallow at all, so she took me to the doctor's. I hate strep. I hate the big shot you get. I can't go anywhere today and tomorrow. Fanny and Sammy and David have to stay AWAY from me. Mom doesn't worry about herself. For some reason, she never gets strep.

I'm in my bed. I have a glass of juice next to me.

Mom brought it up. That's the only good thing about being sick. I can be waited on. I like standing at the top of the stairs and crying out in a pitiful voice, "Mom, can you please get me some juice? My throat hurts." Too bad this only works for one day. I've had strep a few times. I know that on the second day Mom makes me get my own food.

Tomorrow is the Great Sabbath, the Saturday before Passover (which of course you must know, E.). Everyone except the strep-infected one—ME—will go to synagogue and then to Dad. The doctors say that he might be able to come home for the first Seder. He is getting very restless. We have to keep telling him that the bakery is fine. None of us has said that we've been open only half days since Dad went into the hospital. You can only do so much. Meantime, Dad's helpers are selling off all the *chometzdikeh* items. Dad always stays closed over the Passover holiday. Can you imagine what kind of work it takes to make a bakery ready for Passover?

Right now our house looks like a distribution center. If I weren't in this bed, I'd be tripping over the bottles of kosher-for-Passover wine and the boxes of egg and plain matzos near the front door. (Don't come early, E., or you'll have to be careful not to trip over the boxes.) The *shmura matzos*, which Bob Ginzburg ordered, stand near the dining room table because they deserve a better place to wait.

"I imagine Mr. Ginzburg will want us to have him for Pesach this year," said Mom.

Elijah, Dad always invites Bob Ginzburg. It's a family tradition. Like saying the Four Questions or opening the door for you. "He should get married," says Mom. But he never does. "Someone else should invite him," says Sammy. But no one does. Or he doesn't say yes to anyone except us.

Sammy and Fanny and I groan. David doesn't understand the problem. "We'll have to listen to his bad jokes," we say.

"He'll spill wine again this year," says Mom. (Bob Ginzburg always spills wine.)

But he's Dad's friend. It's part of what I love about Dad.

E., there are so many things I *do* love about Dad. Somehow I feel as if I've forgotten to tell you about them.

Dad has all kinds of friends. Some of them are popular. They have everything: money; fine houses; nice clothes; presentable, well-behaved kids; brains—you name it, they've got it. And they like Dad. Dad runs the kosher bakery. People trust him because he's so honest. And you can talk Yiddish with Dad. You can feel your roots way down to the bottom of your feet. And some of these people . . . they don't feel their roots anywhere except in our bakery.

Some of Dad's friends are weird. They chain-smoke and whisper biblical passages as if they were whispering marriage vows. Usually they walk into walls or knock over furniture while they're whispering. They also eat like pigs—with their fingers—and they drive

Mom nuts because they slurp their chicken soup. The last bit which they can't get with their spoons, they get by lifting the bowl up and slurping. Or they take the delicious braided challa that Dad bakes for Shabbes and they tear it up into little bits so there are bread crumbs everywhere. Then they dunk the challa into the soup.

E., these friends of Dad's have no money, or nearly none. "From hand to mouth," that's how they live, at least that's what Dad says. So Dad tries to help them. Dad doesn't give money. He knows his friends. They won't take. Dad drops by their small rented houses with bakery items that he says he would have thrown out because they're getting stale. Or he suddenly sees a buy on oranges. He just had to get a case.

It's all part of my father's expansiveness, E. His heart is like an open door. Even now that it's damaged. He keeps asking Mom if she checked up on Mr. Weinstein and why doesn't she stop by his place and take him out since he doesn't have a car. Then he'll say, "How's the fruit at Costco this week? Take Mr. Weinstein and see if you can find any deals. Tell him how much you saved, so giving him doesn't cost a thing."

And every Passover, Dad invites. Sometimes he invites ten people. They don't all show. But Bob Ginzburg always comes.

"I figured you might be too busy for the Pesach Hershey's Kisses," said Bob Ginzburg when he fell into our house this morning. (E., Bob Ginzburg never walks into our house. He falls in.)

"Thank you," said Mom, waving me back upstairs. (I hate being contagious!)

"I asked your husband if he'd be home this Pesach. They still haven't told him definitely."

Mom nodded.

"Maybe then you'll be having the Seder without him."

Mom nodded again.

"You'll need a leader," said Mr. Ginzburg.

"We'll make do," said Mom, frowning at me. I had almost made it back down to the goodies. "However, you are cordially invited. As our guest."

B.G. bowed forward, or maybe he was just falling, and then he turned around, tripped over the doormat, and fell out the door.

R.

P.S. Did you ever figure out the elephant jokes?

1. *How do you know that an elephant has been in the refrigerator?*
   ANSWER: You can see his footprints in the Jell-O.
2. *How do you know that an elephant is in the elevator with you?*
   ANSWER: You can smell the peanuts on his breath.

April 4—
two more days
until you know what

Dear E.,

I didn't write yesterday. My head hurt too much. I feel better today, though. I'm not contagious, either, although Mom still didn't want me to go to Hebrew school. It's nice missing a Sunday. Then I can sleep late.

It's Palm Sunday today, E., if you aren't up on Christian holidays. This morning I was walking down our block. Mom is letting me walk outside. She just wants me to stay away from people one more day. (By the way, E., nobody else in our family got the strep.) I saw a crowd at St. Mary's, the church on our corner. I've never been inside St. Mary's. Sometimes I wonder what it's like, but I've never been inside. I walked up the stairs once. I let my hand rest on the door. I am going inside one day. I would like to look around.

Next week will be Easter Sunday. If I were Christian I'd think about the Resurrection. How Jesus lay in the tomb and then rose.

Once Ann Johnson, a Christian friend of mine, and I were talking about the Messiah. I don't know how we got started. I guess I was at her house, and I was looking at Christ on the cross. His arms stretched out. His feet twisted. I was thinking how I look but don't get inside. I can't explain it. When I see a Star of David, I look and I'm inside. It's part of me. Just like you're part of me, E., when I'm really thinking and writing. But Christ. He's just there.

I was looking, but I was trying not to stare.

"That's our Messiah," said Ann. You could tell she was inside. And for a second I felt not only outside but left out. But I didn't want to move inside, either. I just liked looking. There are so many things one can wonder about without getting inside of them.

I nodded.

"Do you have a Messiah?"

I nodded. "He hasn't come yet."

"Oh."

We both sat.

"When will he come?" asked Ann.

E., I felt like saying, After lunch, but I knew that wasn't nice, so I kept quiet. Besides, I knew Ann was serious. She really wanted to know. "When the world is ready, and everything is nearly perfect," I said.

"If everything is perfect, why does he need to show up?"

I looked at Ann. She had me there. "I'll have to ask my rabbi," I said. "I don't know."

"What's it like to think the Messiah hasn't come? What's it like to still be waiting?"

"I don't know. I don't think about it much."

"But what's it like not knowing if you're saved or not?"

I wanted to answer, E., but I couldn't because of the language. Remember how I told you about hospital language? When Ann asked me, I realized that she had this language. She had these words she learned at church like I learned words in synagogue, and we didn't know each other's language.

Elijah, when the Messiah comes, will there be only one language?

And would I want that? Wouldn't that be boring?

If Ann and I were the same, she wouldn't be asking me questions. I wouldn't be thinking of my own questions. We wouldn't ever need to ask. Maybe even questions would disappear.

I like questions, E. I like to sit next to Ann and wonder about the mystery of it all.

Yours,
Rebecca

P.S. E., when you look at the Messiah, what do you feel? You have seen him, haven't you? Is the Messiah someone you can really see? Or is he hidden, even from you? And why does he need you? Can't he turn hearts by himself?

Dear E.,

I wish I could hand this in to my teacher, E. I'm doing so poorly in writing. Last year Mrs. Gulbin, who is the absolutely best teacher ever—she's not at all like Bulldog—said, "Rebecca, write what you want." Mrs. Gulbin thinks that you have to find your own subject. It can't be chosen for you all the time. You have to get involved and ask your questions and figure out your answers. She doesn't even believe in a set length. Bulldog has us writing four-paragraph themes all the time. Every essay has to have an introduction, which is one paragraph, a body, which is two paragraphs, and a conclusion, which restates the introduction in another paragraph. But what if what you need to say has to be said in five paragraphs?

"Trust yourself and your topic," said Mrs. Gulbin. "Your work will be as long as it needs to be."

It's hard to follow Mrs. Gulbin's way, E. Sometimes you feel lost. You want someone to tell you what to do. But her way makes sense, even in areas outside of writing. For example, I spend too much time thinking about what I should do and how I'm not doing that. I am going to spend more time thinking about what I'm doing and how that makes me feel. Still, I don't want to hurt anyone. I'm like that, E. I hate to hurt anyone. Maybe I want everyone to love me.

HAVE YOU PACKED YOUR ETERNITY BAG, YET, E.? I AM
GOING TO MISS WRITING TO YOU! YOU ARE A PART OF MY
LIFE!

E., I know you can read my mind, and I don't have
to ask you questions directly. Everything that is really important you'll see. Especially questions about
Dad. But I'm often tired right before you come. What
if I can't remember what I wanted to ask. What if I
open the door, and I see you in all your glory, and I
say, "How old are you?" I can be stupid like that
sometimes.

So I got to thinking that maybe I should write
things down. I want everything to be in my mind
when the mind reading starts.

These are my questions:

1. *Is there really a God?*
2. *Are there many gods, like a God for
   Christians, and a God for Jews, and a God
   for Muslims? Is there one God who
   becomes whatever God you'd like Him to
   be? You know, sort of like a quick-change
   artist?*
3. *What does the Messiah look like?*
4. *What grade will I get in math this year?*
5. *Will I get married, and will my husband be
   ugly? Will he be some ugly man who loves
   tongue and boiled beef?*
6. *I know I'm Jewish, but what does that
   mean? I mean . . . if I were Christian, and I*

*were looking up at Christ, what would I
feel?*

7. *Elijah, who is the most interesting person
   you've ever met?*
8. *What will I be when I grow up?*
9. *Will I ever be twenty years old?*
10. *Do you ever wear shoes on your journeys?
    Why can't a girl be a messenger? I'm sure
    there are messenger shoes in girl sizes, too.*
11. *Can I come with you?*
12. *Can you make Dad's heart well?*
13. *Can you bring him back the way he was?
    Happy.*
14. *Would it help if I prayed? If I prayed to
    God, would it help?*

Rebecca

Monday, April 5—
before school

Dear Chariot Rider, Eternity Traveler, Confidant,
Friend, Messianic Messenger, Mr. Big Cheese,
Eliyahu Ha-Navi, Son of Someone, the Invisible
One, E.,

TOMORROW IS THE FIRST NIGHT OF PASSOVER! You
might be able to borrow a used broom if the chariot is
beyond repair. Or somebody might have a starship

somewhere. Otherwise, you can think your way into time present. Just close your eyes, E. Think matzo balls. *Do not think tongue!*

Today we started the countdown. E., it was as if we were all at the Kennedy Space Center, except we were about to launch the Spirit of Passover. Mom and Sammy and Fanny and David and I, we all began bumping into each other, in between our bumping into boxes of things. We are a very mad bunch right before Passover.

After school, Mom gathered all us kids in the kitchen. We stood in front of her while she stared down at us. There was that look on her face. (Mom has this "look," E., which she gets right before major holidays.) Nearly every disaster was written in that look. The Seder plate is broken or can't be found. The wine has spilled over the whole tablecloth. A slice of bread drops out of a dining room drawer, and some guest spies it. The matzo balls don't rise. Passover doesn't come at all. Or worse yet, Passover does come, but it skips the Samuelson house and lands on another instead.

Mom sighed. We all stood across from her and made a communal sigh.

Then Mom straightened her shoulders and became the other Passover Mom. The leader capable of sending us into combat. The five-star general. The commander in chief. We rallied around her.

"You," Mom said, "you clear out all the high cupboards and see if you can locate my Pesach Mix-master. It's in the attic somewhere." Mom tapped Sammy on the shoulder.

Sammy turned sharply and strode into action.

"You," she said, tapping Fanny, "you make large strips of aluminum foil so we can line the refrigerator after I've cleaned it."

Fanny nodded. It was a very small nod. Let's face it, E., a person who thinks she is Joseph-the-moon or Joseph-the-sun doesn't take commands well, even on Passover.

"You," said Mom, giving me her stern no-nonsense look, "you find the good Pesach tablecloth in the dining room china cabinet. Also, cut up pieces of this shelf paper to line the cupboards."

"And you," she said, looking at my little brother, "you help out your brother and sisters."

We bowed our heads. We felt as if Mom was not only a commander in chief, she was the royal queen as well, and she had knighted us all. It was our knightly duty to save Queen Mom and King Dad from the armies of *chometzdikeh* goods: bread and cereal and cracker crumbs crumpled inside of cellophane wrappers, old stale gum someone had left in a drawer once, half of a lollipop stuck inside my spring jacket pocket.

We galloped through the house. We dumped our clothes onto the floor. We combed through our bureaus and closets. When one of us found a *chometz-*

71

dikeh item, that person shouted, "Found it!" You'd have thought we were playing *Jeopardy!* or Bingo or *Wheel of Fortune*, and Vanna White was wheeling in the hot prizes. David got so excited he kept screaming, "Found it!" even when he hadn't found anything except some loose change or cuff links.

Then, while David was napping, Mom and Fanny and Sammy and I brought down the Passover dishes from their attic storage place. I dusted the bowls I love: the white bowls with red circles on them that look like cherries without stems.

I held the green milk dishes in my hands. Our kosher-for-Passover milk dishes aren't any prettier than our regular dishes, but somehow they seem special. Passover special. Once-a-year special. Old and new all at the same time.

I closed my eyes. I could smell the food. I could taste Passover.

Monday—
before dinner

E.,

You know I had a busy day, and I felt tired. When David woke up from his nap, I took one. I never sleep during the day. I can't fall asleep when it's still light outside. But I fell asleep today because of the strep and all. And I had a dream. About you. This is sort of how I remember it.

You and I are seated at the dining room table. It's Passover night, so all the symbols are around us. You're sitting on your special chair near your own special silver cup. I'm across from you. We're leaning on big fat pillows just the way Dad leans on Passover night.

But Dad isn't in my dream. None of the family is there. Even Mr. Ginzburg isn't around. Just you and me.

You have a big pack of cards in front of you, and you're dressed like some gangster. You wear a black trench coat and a black hat. And you're smoking a cigar. You are also shuffling cards as if you've been shuffling all your eternal life.

We're playing War. I don't know why. That's such a baby game. Even David can play War. But this is a dream, so I'm not my usual intelligent self. *Hah!*

You deal me half the deck and keep the other half.

"No peeking," you say.

"I just want to see how many high cards I have."

"Against the rules. You'll see when you turn the cards over."

"I bet you have all the aces." I straighten my pile. You smile.

I turn over my first card. "Queen," I shout, watching you bend your card so only you can see it. "Not

73

fair," I say, shaking my head. "We have to turn the cards together. *The rules!*"

You grunt and turn over a three.

I smile.

You whip out an ace. "Knew it," I whisper. I have a measly six. "At least you didn't get a high card," I add.

We both put down tens. We look at each other. "W . . . A . . . R," we chant, each slowly putting three cards facedown below the tens.

"You show yours first!" I say.

"You first!" You take a big puff on your cigar. A big smoky "E" forms above your head.

"You shouldn't smoke," I say. "It's bad for your lungs."

"Alcohol's no good, either, so why do you keep offering it to me."

We lay our cards down together. We both have kings. Kings of hearts.

"Something's wrong with the deck," I say. "You can't have two kings of the same suit."

You smile again, and suddenly the hearts start pumping. "You want to play some more?" you ask, tapping your cigar. The ashes fall onto the cards and vanish instantly.

I nod.

You take off your hat. On your head is a yarmulkah held down by a black bobby pin. You mop your brow with a big hankie. There is a capital "E" on the

74

hankie. (I bet you have "E"s on your bath towels, too.) "I like a girl with spunk," you say, waving one hand over the hearts. They stop pumping. Then you tap the edge of the table. "The Messiah's messenger has many tricks up his sleeve," you say.

I stare at your fingers. They are pudgy. There is black hair on your knuckles. Your hands seem to shrink and even disappear. "Who needs hands?" you whisper.

Your cup seems to float in the air. And your hands reappear, holding it. "I bet you can't do that," you say, readjusting the bobby pin. "How much time did it take?"

"I wasn't counting."

"I seem to get slower and slower." You sip the wine. "Manischewitz," you say, smacking your lips. "Cherry."

"What about Mogen David?"

"Last year it was Mogen David." You swirl the wine in your cup. And you sip slowly. "This year I have a sweet tooth. So it's Manischewitz Cherry."

I watch your lips touching the silver, but nothing disappears.

"You think that's good?" you say, your gold crown glinting.

"Not as good as the disappearing. It seems easy."

"You want to try?"

"Can you teach me?"

"Too young for wine. Maybe in a few years."

75

You lean over and tap on my corner of the table. A glass filled with liquid appears before me. "Drink," you say. "It's Welch's. White grape."

Then suddenly you get serious. You're still smiling, but it's a prophetic smile. The kind where I can't see your teeth. "Let's quit," you say. "I'm tired."

"But I'm winning."

"I'll let you win." You sip your wine noiselessly. Then you tilt your whole cup. The wine doesn't spill, even while you drink.

I lift my glass.

"You'll spill," you say, shaking your head.

"No I won't."

"Yes you will."

I turn my glass over above my mouth. The white grape juice slides down my face and onto my lap.

"I never say I told you so." You chuckle a deep chuckle while you tap the table, and I'm completely dry again.

"It saves laundry expenses," you say, leaning over and patting my cheek. "Imagine the kind of laundry a guy who travels through eternity needs."

"Let's finish. I hate winning by default."

"Tired," you say, so softly I can hardly hear. Then you look at me, E. But you're not looking at me. You're looking inside of me into places even I can't see. The room where we play is still and silent, while your eyes just seem to travel across the miles between us. And I know.

76

I know you've ridden in the fiery chariot.

I know you've been pulled by the flaming horses.

I know how you cried when you watched Elisha, even while you said, "Take the cloak. Take the cloak." You didn't want to go. Nobody does. Not even someone who knows he'll become the Messiah's messenger.

"Do you know," you say, coming over to me and touching my hair gently, "do you know, Rebeccaleh, how often I've asked him to come? Do you know how often I've begged?"

I shake my head.

"You don't know what begging is. You have no idea."

Tears well up from somewhere deep inside my body. I could flood the world with the way I feel. But I don't want you to see. I want you to think I have spunk. "Why doesn't he come?" I say, forcing the words out of my chest. I sound like a crow, cawing.

"Too much strife."

"Why doesn't he come and fix it?"

"Why don't you fix things for yourself!" you shout at me, and your words feel like fire.

"If we could fix everything, then why would we even need him?" I shout back. I am amazed at my own spunk.

"To ask when there is no need . . . Do you know how he'd feel?" You touch my cheek. "Have you ever,'' you ask in a voice that's as gentle as a feather, ''Rebeccaleh, have you ever loved anybody?''

Tears run down my face. I pretend it's not me who's crying.

You sit down, smack the fat pillows, and lean back again. ''I'll tell you,'' you say, your voice sounding wearier than any voice I've ever heard, ''I am sick to death of Mogen David and I am sick to death of Manischewitz. I hate wine. Once, just once, I would like someone to leave out a good hot cup of strong tea. I would also like a bed. After all these millions of miles, who needs a straight-backed chair. Elegance, schmelegance. Tea. Some crackers. And a bed.''

''You can't have crackers.'' I feel very mean-spirited. ''No crackers allowed on Pesach.''

''That, too, I'm sick to death of. I'm sick to death of Pesach. A plague on it. It is easy for you, a young thing like you. But me? How many times do you think I've heard the Exodus story? Guess. How many?''

''A million?''

You shake your head.

''A trillion?''

Your tongue makes clucking sounds.

''A quatrillion?''

''No such word. But who cares. I just ask you how many times can one man listen to the Pesach story? The same adventure over and over again. The same Four Questions. The same plagues. The same hard-

78

hearted Pharaoh. The drowning. The wandering. The 'It would have been enough.' Even the 'One kid, one kid that Father bought.' Always the man buys one kid. Can't he think of something else?''

"I thought you appeared at the end of the Seder.''

"Sometimes I come early. Then I get bored waiting outside. I get very bored. I'm sick to death of it all.''

"I always liked the Four Questions,'' I say to myself. "I like the asking and the answering. The sameness.''

You pound your fist on the table. Cards scatter all over. "I want a fantasy book next to my bed!'' you scream. "I want Tolkien or Lloyd Alexander. Or Madeleine L'Engle, I like her. The IT who controls everything, that's frightening. It's fresh. It's new. Forget the Exodus. Give me the wicked brain. Also crackers. And hot tea. And the bed. I like to read in bed. Better yet, I like to be read to. Don't you think I deserve that? Why can't somebody read to me while I rest on a bed and eat my crackers and lie back on a pillow? Two pillows. Why can't someone else be the messenger for a change? Why can't someone else wait to lead him in? I'm sick to death of waiting, too. And of begging. Who needs the Messiah? I ask you, who needs him!''

I look down at my hands. I want to speak, but I'm tired. So very tired. I feel terribly sad, too. "I'll read to you,'' I say. "I'm a good reader.''

You laugh that low, throaty laugh of yours. "Don't

pay any attention to me," you say. "I get overexcited. Really, I like my job. Really."

You clap your hands together. Your cup disappears. So does my glass. The cards disappear. The table disappears. Even the chairs are gone. We stand across from each other.

"Do you want me to make you disappear?" you ask, grinning slyly.

"Where would I go?"

"Who knows?"

"Could I come back?"

"Who knows?"

I shake my head. I feel like a coward.

You pat me on the shoulder. Your hand feels warm. "You made a good choice. You are wise. You are also kind. Now, since I forfeited the game, even though I was in the lead, you can ask me anything. Only about the afterlife you're not allowed to ask. Other than that, anything at all."

I think about anything. There is so much, so much to ask. Anything is too much.

I blurt out, "How old are you?"

Dear E.,

IT'S TONIGHT, E.! THE NIGHT WE'VE BEEN WAITING
FOR! And Mom did it all. I never thought she could.
Dad always pushed. He always supervised. But this
year Mom did it, and we're ready.

Last night we made the final check. After supper,
Mom gathered Sammy, Fanny, David, and me in the
kitchen. "Your father," said Mom, "would like to see
us do this all so when he comes home, he will come
home to a Pesach house."

The doctors say, E., he'll come home soon. Not in
time for the Seder, but soon. And then we'll take him
to Philadelphia, where they will give him a bypass.
And he will be as good as new. He will be better than
he was before. Just as long as the surgery goes right.

And I do want him home, E. I want him home very
much. I have things to tell him. You have to do that
with Dad. You have to tell him how it is in your own
world, even if that hurts him. You have to tell him
how you're making a place for yourself. Like with
prayer. You're finding your own route.

I have been thinking about praying, E. I have been
thinking about all those prayers I said when I was
little. They made me feel good. I'm just not ready
yet. I want the words to feel right. From inside of me.
I want to feel right.

Last night Mom gave each of us some pieces of stale bread. She smiled at us. You could tell she was nervous.

"You're doing fine," said Sammy.

"Maybe it's not the way your father does it," said Mom.

"I like the way you do it," I said. "I like the way both of you do it."

I took David's hand and started up the stairs.

"Here," I whispered to David, "put the bread here." We stuck a piece of bread behind Mom's bedroom mirror. "Don't make crumbs," I said. David giggled. Fanny and Sammy ran up and down, pushing each other. "Stop following me!" yelled Sammy.

"Fart face!" screamed Fanny.

"Fat fanny! Fat fanny!"

"Sick Sammy. Stupid Sammy. Mucous-membrane brain."

David parked himself across from the fighting pair. "Walla-Walla-Washington!" he screamed, hitting the air with his fists. I could tell he wanted someone to fight. Maybe the tension in the house was becoming too much for him.

"A face only a mother could love on payday!" said Sammy, contorting his face and wiggling around Fanny.

"Mucous-membrane brain," repeated Fanny. "Pea brain. Dinosaur brain!"

"Bad breath in dogs," said Sammy, shoving his face up against Fanny's.

"Walla-Walla-Washington!" David jumped up and down like a monkey. "Walla-Walla-Washington!"

Mom's voice galloped up the stairs behind us. "Can't you all stop!" she shouted. We all fell silent. We knew Mom was hunched in a kitchen chair. Torn sheets of paper were strewn everywhere around her. We could hear her making her last list. "Brillo pads," she was muttering. "A shank bone for the Seder plate. A roasted egg."

Our feet pounded the stairs. We felt the way you do when you play hide-and-seek: excited and anxious. We turned corners at breakneck speed.

Finally we all collected ourselves back in the kitchen, which Mom had made dark. She held a candle in one hand. In the other she held a long white feather, a wooden spoon, and a paper plate.

"Walla-Walla-Washington," whispered David, poking me with his bony little-boy elbows.

"Shh," I whispered back. I stared at the wall. Thin shadows spotted the daisies that seemed to touch and then separate.

Then we moved into the dark spaces of our house. *Bedikat Chometz.* The search for *chometz.* We stole silently behind Mom, directing her from the back. I imagined bread cowering in corners. "Look!" whispered Sammy loudly. "Look here, Dad."

Sammy caught his breath. Mom touched his shoulder. Then she lowered the candle. Wax dripped onto her hand. In my mind I could see Dad's hairy hand next to Mom's. Sammy held the spoon while the feather brushed against the leavened bread. Then Sammy dumped the bread pieces from the spoon onto the paper plate.

Bedikat Chometz. Our shoes whispered the words. Our eyes were black hawk eyes. Nothing escaped us. Even David was silent. I could hear it in his mind: Walla-Walla . . . But he wasn't saying anything.

"Here's another," said Fanny, beating Sammy to it. We led Mom to a bureau and then behind a mirror. The feather swooped down again, gathering the bread David and I had hidden.

Early this morning Mom and Sammy and Fanny and David and I went out to the backyard. Mom lit a match, and we watched the *chometz* burning. Our souls felt burned clean, and they wanted to sing sweet Passover songs.

Why are these eight days different from all other days? On all other days we walk around with leavened-bread bodies. But on Passover we have hard, crunchy matzo bodies.

Right after lunch, a man came with a blowtorch and burned our oven clean. And our house became a Passover house. A changed house.

Dear E.,

I didn't want to tell anyone how it all happened—
not even you. I didn't want to talk about it. But now
I do.

Dad came home late from work one night. We were
all sleeping. There was a thump in the kitchen. I
heard it, and Mom heard it, and Fanny heard it. David
and Sammy sleep through anything.

Dad was on the floor near the phone. The back of
his head had been cut. It was on the floor all over.
Dad's blood.

Then Mom was leaning over him. Sammy had
come downstairs and called for the ambulance. The
paramedics were telling him what Mom was supposed to do. Sammy was telling Mom, and Mom kept
screaming, "Is this right? Is this right?" even while
she was pressing down.

Mom saved Dad's life, E. She doesn't say that,
though. She talks about the when and the how and
the way minutes seemed like hours, as we waited for
the ambulance. She doesn't say how she pressed
down even while she kept screaming at Sammy, "Is
this right? Is this right?"

My mother's world is a very quiet world, E. It's not
like Dad's at all, and sometimes I forget that she has

her own world, a world where she's just herself. Lately, though, I've been seeing how she makes her own spaces.

When I grow up, E., I do not want to be just like my mother. Or my father. But I would like to see them in me. I would like to look at myself in the mirror and see them. And me.

Right now, though, I need to see me. And I need to know they're right behind me, Mom and Dad.

I want them both to see me, changing.

April 6—
the first Seder

Dear E.,

I am not at the Seder. Nobody knows where I am. I don't even know if I should tell you, but you probably know. I thought of going to St. Mary's. I even opened the door, but it was the wrong place. So here I am in the synagogue.

I knew I'd get in, E., because the janitor's always in the synagogue. His second home. That's what the congregation says. The gossips say he must be unhappy with his own home, and that's why he has a cot in his supply room. But most of us know. We know that he has found a private space in this place. Inside the synagogue, in his own supply room, he sits and reads, and it doesn't matter that he's not Jewish. How could God care, E.? Even if Norman, our janitor, wanted to pray to Jesus inside the synagogue, why would God care? Because the synagogue is Norman's house, too. Norman's the one who painted the walls of the Hebrew school, and when anything needs fixing, Norman fixes it. I bet Norman knows places in this synagogue nobody knows about, not even the rabbi. So why should God care?

That's why I knew I could get in. Anyone who wants to just sit here can usually sit. You knock on the outside door, and Norman comes. He doesn't ask you what you want. He smiles. Then he goes back to whatever he was doing. And it's comforting. It's comforting to feel him there.

Sometimes I wish, E., I wish the whole world could sit here.

I brought my binder here, E. At first I didn't want to take it. I wanted to run and run, but my binder makes me feel good, too, E. A part of me is inside here. A part of you is inside here.

I like sitting here in the main sanctuary. When I was five I came here, and we had a consecration service. I got a little Torah. It looked almost like the one we have in synagogue. You could open it using the small wooden scrolls. And all Five Books of Moses were in it. Except the print was very tiny. I still have it. And the rabbi took a large tallis and stretched it over all of us kids.

"You are about to begin your formal Jewish education," Rabbi Shapiro said. Next year he'll say the same thing to David. I know he will, and I know how, when he says it, I'll want to cry because I will remember how I heard the same thing.

I'm sitting in the back, where Mom and Fanny and I always sit for Yom Kippur, the holiest of holidays. When we fast and remember our past bad deeds and cleanse our souls for the Jewish New Year. Mom and Fanny and I like to sit in the back and listen to the sounds of the long blast of the shofar, echoing through the aisles when the holiday ends. We like to be behind everyone. Quiet in our own worlds.

And I have seen Dad read from the Torah here. Fanny had her Bat Mitzvah. Sammy had his Bar Mitzvah. It has all happened right here. And next year, right before I turn thirteen, I'll have my Bat Mitzvah. Some of the girls in our congregation do it at age twelve, E. I wanted to wait until I'm thirteen.

I'll stand at the pulpit, and my family will watch me. Fanny will be thinking about all the wonderful presents I got. They'll be much better than hers. And David will be there, looking older. And my mother will be there. She will be very proud. And Sammy. And Dad . . . He will not be a thin dad, E. He will look like my dad.

Sometimes, E., I even imagine myself being married here. When I stretch my mind out into the future. But I've never sat here alone, like this, on Seder

88

night, when you should be sitting with your whole family and talking about the Exodus. I've never sat all alone.

Mom and Fanny and David and Sammy and Mr. Ginzburg must have started the Seder. After I ran out, they must have started. Everyone's at home. Except me. And Norman. We're in the synagogue. And Dad. He's back in intensive care.

When I stretch my mind out as far as it will go, E., I imagine my whole family in the wedding party. Fanny doesn't like her dress, but she's there, smiling. And Mom is helping me with my veil. Dad is waiting to lead me to my husband. That's the way it is supposed to be, E. Just the way I've always imagined it.

I'm writing in my decorated notebook, E. Tomorrow you can take it with you. For the second Seder. You can read it while you ride the chariot. Dear Elijah . . . here I am in the synagogue, and I don't understand. Everything was going along so well. We were doing our best at everything. This afternoon Mom and I had a matzo-ball-making contest. Mom's came out round and fluffy like full moons. Mine were hard little circles full of pointy goose bumps. Then all of us ran around like chickens with their heads cut off. We fixed the Seder plate. We made *charoseth.* We got the knives and the soup dishes and plates and the Passover wineglasses together. We even polished your silver cup, Elijah. And all of it was going to the hospital.

We had discussed the whole thing with Dad. If the doctors said that he had to stay in the hospital a few more days, then we'd have the Seder in the hospital. And we'd bring everything. Maybe we'd even bring Elijah.

I said that, E. I told Dad that I would open the door to his room because it doesn't matter which door. And you would come. Right into his hospital room.

Will you still do that, E.? Even if I'm here, will you still come to our house and to the hospital?

They must be at the Four Questions now. At home. Mom and Fanny and Sammy and David are doing the full Seder at home because now they can't go to the hospital tonight. I can't go, either. I'm here with you . . . dear E. . . . .

I'm sitting here in the synagogue, and I'm not home, and I'm not in the hospital because of what just happened. The doctors said no visitors, not even Mom. Mom's trying to make it like every other Seder. She's trying to do what Dad would have done.

It'll be a long Seder. It's eight now. I've been here a half hour, and the Seder will go on and on, maybe even until eleven, just like every year, just like we always do.

I want things to be normal again, E. I don't want a mother who is a mother and a father.

So he doesn't know the real me, the one who isn't the Shabbes Princess. He doesn't know how the prayers get stuck in my throat or about all the accidentally-on-purpose things I've done because I'm trying to find my own way. But so what, E.? Who knows anybody, anyway? I hardly know myself. I don't feel mad anymore. And I'm not scared about talking to Dad. About losing his love. Because I'll never lose his love. Maybe he'll just love me differently because he'll see . . . he'll see that I'm not just his daughter, and maybe that will make him scared. Scared for me. And even angry. But that's okay.

Oh, E., I can't wait to sit down with him and tell him. In my way. I love my father, E. I love to hear him say his prayers. No one can say the prayers as fast as Dad. I love it when he pounds the table with his fist when he prays after Shabbes meals. He gets so involved. I love to go into the bakery and know it's his. And when we have our long talk, he'll understand. Or maybe he won't. But that, too, will be all right. Right now I want him home.

E., did you ever wonder about your dad? You must have had a dad. Did you love him, E.? I don't know if he'll ever be the way he was, E. He's back in intensive care. And he's so weak. The hospital called. And Mom ran down. Then she came home, and she said that we had to do the whole thing at home, so we should get started. And I wanted to. I really did.

But I don't like to cry on Passover. Not at the Passover table. Not when we're talking about freedom. Not when everything reminds me of other years. And this year is so, so different. I don't like being sad.

I ran. And I came here. And Norman answered.

And I walked into the main sanctuary. And I sat. And I started writing because I don't know what else to do anymore.

I'm sure Bob Ginzburg is with Mom. He's spilling wine all over the table and he's telling one of his bad jokes. They always start the same: "There was a rabbi, and a priest, and a minister . . ."

I can see it all in my mind. Mom isn't skipping a thing.

I will think about other years. Other Passover years. When we're all together, Dad and Mom and Sammy and Fanny and David and I. We are filling a bowl full of water and salt. Later we'll dip parsley into the bowl. We'll remember spring and tears. Sammy and Fanny and I and David and Mom and Dad—we will taste slavery in our mouths.

E., a Passover house is full of history. History and mystery. And I am seven and I am eight and I am nine and I am filled with expectation. When Elijah comes, I think, the neighbors' dog won't bark the way he usually does when he sees strangers. He will know it's Elijah. He'll wag his tail.

And when I open the door . . .

David sings the Four Questions. Really he just hums along with me because he's so little. Or he says, "Old MacDonald *Mashtanah* E-I-E-I-O." David's voice is like a blade of grass I suck on in the spring. It's high and reedy. Mine is lower. Sammy sings after David and I do. He sings in Hebrew and Yiddish and

English. Sometimes David breaks in with a "Moo-moo here," and we laugh.

Then Fanny sings a new version we've never heard before. Fanny always knows new things. She sings in her Fanny-dramatic voice. She sings well. She should be the Shabbes Princess, I think. But for some reason that's the way Dad sees me. Even if I were born on Sunday and hadn't broken any rules, he'd see me that way. I wonder if my husband will be that blind. Part of me would want it that way. Part of me wouldn't.

We come to the Four Sons. Fanny wants to be the Wise Son. So do I. "Last year," I scream, "I was the *tam*! I was the Simple Son! I can't be a *tam* every year."

"You are a *tam*!" screams Fanny, sticking out her warty-pickle tongue.

"*Shah!*" whispers Dad loudly. "*Shah!*" He points to David, who gets to be the Wise Son, even though he's so little he can hardly speak.

And then, as it does every year, Passover enters through our ears. We hear our voices saying the prayers. Passover enters through our noses. We smell matzo balls and chicken soup and roast turkey. Passover enters through our mouths. We can even feel it in our bones.

Oh, E., being Jewish, E., it's like a whole people being stitched together. With the threads holding. And there are tons of things I don't know. Like what if the whole world could stitch itself together? All the races? What if the dead could come back to life? What

93

if the bad could become good and there was no hunger? What if the Messiah came? And all the questions were answered?

What if I am always sad, and Dad's heart stops mending? And I don't care about change anymore? And I never find the right man? What if I don't ever marry, and I don't have a family, and I am very old? All by myself at the Seder table. Would you come to me then, Elijah? When I opened the door, would you come?

I want to open the door, Elijah. I want to keep opening it. But what if, what if when I am old and gray I stop opening? Dear Elijah, Mr. Messenger, Chariot Rider, Ha-Navi, E., what if I stop? Will you still come then? Mr. Turner of Hearts, will you fly around the world with me through an eternity of time? And then will you lay your body across the whole of the universe?

April 20

Dear Elijah,

As you might have guessed, Passover is over. And I haven't been writing. I wanted to tell you that David and I bought a second pair of slippers for Dad. They'll be his bakery slippers, so we've left them there. Near the front door. When he walks in, he'll see them.

I haven't forgotten you. I will never forget, especially that night in the synagogue.

It was you, wasn't it? Except you had on one of your disguises, so you looked different. You looked like someone who comes every year to our Seder, someone who spills wine and keeps falling over things.

I should have guessed you wouldn't come as a prince.

I know it was you.

But it doesn't matter.

It seemed like forever that I was in that synagogue, E. But it probably was only an hour, wasn't it?

Did Norman open the door? And who did Norman see, E.? Do you think he saw you, too?

I will always remember, E. I turned around and I saw. On the outside I saw someone who looked like Bob Ginzburg.

He came through the back of the sanctuary. He was tripping, too, E. He was tripping over the rug. Then he sat down next to me.

You sat down.

"I've been writing you letters," I whispered. "Long letters."

"Your family is waiting for me," you said. Or maybe you said, "Your family is waiting for you." Your voice sounded like Bob Ginzburg's voice.

"Did they open the door yet?" I asked.

"David did it."

"I wanted to open it," I said.

"It's no longer necessary," you answered. You sat next to me in the synagogue. Your hands were in your coat pockets. In Mr. Ginzburg's pockets. I could hear the cards being shuffled. I could even hear the horses neighing.

"It's time to come home. To sing 'One kid, one kid that Father bought.' "

"I thought you were tired of that song."

"Who said that?" You winked at me.

"Sammy found the *afikoman*, didn't he?" Sammy always finds it unless Mom makes Dad give the rest of us hints.

"Your brother hid it this year. He hid it so good that he can't remember where it is."

"That's my favorite part of the evening."

"Mine, too."

"I also like the Four Questions, I'll have you know. And all the other business."

"So come home. Your mother needs you. She's worried."

You took my hand. We didn't fly around the world, E. We didn't fly through eternity. We just walked together out of the synagogue, and as we walked . . .

Oh, E., as we walked, I started praying.

And I'm still doing that. Right now, with Dad in Philadelphia, with Mom waiting outside the operating room, I'm praying.

"Please, God, make my dad well."

Afikoman. Before the Seder meal, the leader breaks a matzo and hides the larger half. Children always try to spy out where the *afikoman* is hidden, and they have to wait through the whole Seder before beginning the search. Traditionally, the child who finds this piece of matzo gets to bargain it off for a reward. The Seder cannot conclude until every member has had a piece of the *afikoman.*

Bar Mitzvah. When a Jewish boy reaches thirteen, a ceremony is held, signaling the fact that the boy has become "a man" and can now assume duties that traditionally have been accorded to Jewish men.

Bat Mitzvah. Some synagogues have introduced Bat Mitzvahs to signal maturation for girls. Often these occur at age twelve. They can also occur at age thirteen, depending on the synagogue's calendar.

Bedikat Chometz. The search for leaven before Passover, a ritual performed the evening before the first Seder. Traditionally, families search by candlelight for the bread that has been left in various places and sweep the crumbs with a feather into a wooden spoon. The crumbs are kept until the next morning, when they are burned.

Challa. A loaf of delicious white bread, sometimes sweetened a little, and braided on top. Challa is eaten on the Sabbath and on holidays.

Chometz. Anything that is leavened and not permitted in observant households on Passover. (*Chometzdik; chometzdikeh:* adj.)

Exodus, Book of. The second book of the Torah, which describes how the Jews were held in Egypt as slaves, and how they were delivered out of their bondage by God. The mass departure of the Jews from Egypt is called the Exodus.

Four Questions. These are preceded by *Mah Nishtanah Ha-leilah Ha-zeh Mekol Ha-leilot,* or "Why is this night different from all other nights?" Traditionally, the youngest child present at the Seder table asks the father the questions in song. During the Seder, the father recounts the answers in lengthy detail as all present participate in the telling of the Exodus story. The questions, loosely translated, are:

1. On all other nights we may eat either leavened bread or unleavened. Why on this night do we eat only unleavened?
2. On all other nights we eat all manner of herbs. Why on this night do we eat only those that are bitter?
3. On all other nights we do not steep (or dip) that which we eat even once. Why on this night do we steep twice?
4. On all other nights we eat either sitting or reclining. Why on this night do all recline?

The father's reply to the Four Questions begins with the memory of bondage in Egypt, God's deliverance, and one's duty to recount the story so that freedom may always be cherished. Because the child's questions lead to this retelling upon which the entire Seder ritual hinges, the child's role is seen as most important.

Four Sons. A portion of the Passover Seder reading (from the *Haggadah*), often said by the children of the household. The four sons represent ways in which children approach the meaning of the Seder, and include the Wise Son, the Wicked Son, the Simple Son, and the Son Who Doesn't Know How to Ask. Often boys and girls will tease one another about who is who. The *tam* is the Simple Son.

Haggadah. The special book read during the Passover Seder. It contains the narrative of Israel's slavery and

99

escape from Egypt, and includes songs and anecdotes and words of the sages. The recitation of the story comes from the biblical injunction: "That thou mayest remember the day when thou camest forth out of the land of Egypt all the days of thy life."

"It would have been enough." Choral line from "Dayenu," a song sung during the Passover Seder. One line is "Had He bestowed the Sabbath on us, and not brought us to Mount Sinai, it would have been enough." The line after it is "Had He brought us to Mount Sinai, and not given us the Torah, it would have been enough." By the end of the song, the singers have enumerated more than a dozen reasons for thankfulness.

Kosher. Acceptable to eat according to the dietary laws. Those observing strict dietary rules eat only meat and poultry slaughtered in a specified way (kosher meat). Meat from an animal that does not have a split hoof or chew its cud is unkosher. Meat from a pig is forbidden. Also unkosher is fish without fins or scales (such as shrimp or lobster). Besides this, milk and meat products cannot be eaten together, and a certain number of hours must pass before one can eat milk products after eating meat.

Kosher for Passover (Kosher for Pesach). Usually such an item will have a label on it, indicating that it has not been in contact with *chometz.*

Matzo. Unleavened bread. Tradition has it that the Israelites, in their haste to leave Egypt, had no time to let their bread rise. They took with them the bread that had not risen. Eating unleavened bread, or matzo, reminds Jews of the Exodus. The matzo, a flat kind of bread, has also taken on the aspect of being a bread of humility or a bread of affliction. During Passover, Jews remember the poor and those who are still enslaved. Many Jews also eat *shmura matzo,* special handmade matzo produced in Israel. And many soften matzo in milk or boiled water, mix it with beaten eggs, and fry it to make a breakfast dish called *matzo brei,* which is often eaten with jelly or applesauce.

Messiah. From *mashiach,* or "the anointed one." In early times, Hebrew priests, just like Near East kings, were anointed by having olive oil, a symbol of purity, poured over their heads. Later, the *mashiach* came to be defined as the divinely appointed redeemer, the Messiah. He is perceived as a human and not a divine figure. But when he will come, and who he will be, has always been a subject of conjecture and debate. During the ceremony performed at the end of the Sabbath, many Jews sing *Eliyahu Ha-Navi,* Elijah the Prophet, a song that speaks of the longing for the Messiah, who will be led in by Elijah and will be descended from King David. With the coming of the Messiah, the broken world will be whole again. Mod-

101

ern, liberal Judaism has moved away from a belief in a personal redeemer. Rather, it is thought that one day there will be a Messianic Age, in which all peoples will be united, and wholeness will be achieved through human enterprise, divinely inspired.

"One kid, one kid." Another song sung near the conclusion of the Seder, which, through a cumulative process, extols the power of God over even the Angel of Death.

Passover (Pesach). The festival of Passover revolves around the recalling of Israel's ancient bondage in Egypt, the Exodus, and the receipt of the Ten Commandments. It is a spring holiday centering on the importance of freedom and symbolizing renewal and rebirth.

Seder. Meaning "order," the Seder is the ordered, traditional Passover ritual, which begins with the sanctification of the feast day and moves through such practices as handwashing, eating parsley dipped in salt water, dividing the matzo, reciting the *Haggadah,* and partaking of the meal. The precise order can be found in a *Haggadah.* In the United States there are eight days of Passover, during which only unleavened foods are eaten. The first two nights are Seder nights, when the *Haggadah* is read. In Israel (as well as in some homes in the United States), there is only one Seder night and seven days of Passover. The Seder's focus is the child, who first starts with the

Four Questions and is to hear the answers so that the story can be passed on to subsequent generations.

Seder plate. Prepared before the Seder. The Seder plate can be a very ornate, decorative object, or it can be a simple plate. Several foods, each used during the Seder, are placed on the Seder plate and have symbolic meanings. The following are on most plates:

Karpas. A green vegetable such as parsley or celery. Near the beginning of the Seder this is dipped into salt water. The water symbolizes the tears of those in bondage. The vegetable symbolizes spring and renewal.

Maror. A bitter herb, usually horseradish. This symbolizes the bitterness felt by the Jews in slavery.

Chazeret. Another bitter herb, such as romaine lettuce, because "herbs" are mentioned in the Bible.

Charoseth. A favorite on the Seder plate, made from fruit, nuts, and wine. This represents the bricks and mortar made by Jewish slaves to build Pharaoh's cities. Mixed together in a matzo sandwich, the bitter herbs and the *charoseth* combine the bitterness of slavery with the sweetness of redemption.

Zeroah. A roasted shank bone representing the paschal lamb sacrificed long ago in the Holy Temple before the Pesach festival.

Baytzah. A roasted egg. Symbol of the festival

offering brought to the Holy Temple. Also symbolic of renewal and spring.

Shabbes. The Jewish Sabbath, or day of rest, which begins just before sunset on Friday night and extends to sunset on Saturday night. Some Jews spend the Sabbath in worship and in rest. They do not ride in cars, write, make phone calls, turn on electrical appliances, and so on. Some Jews light Shabbes candles. (The woman of the house performs this ceremony, which inaugurates the Sabbath.) They have a special Friday night dinner, but write and ride and do what is done on other days. Customs vary. In Israel, most shops and markets are closed. However, there, too, religious observances vary.

Shabbes Queen, or Sabbath Queen (technically also called the Sabbath Bride). Tradition has it that the Sabbath Queen or Bride enters into Jewish homes with the lighting of the candles and blesses their homes. *Shabbes Princess,* which derives from *Shabbes Queen,* is a term of endearment sometimes given to daughters.

Shofar. Ram's horn, which is blown in the synagogue during Rosh Hashanah and Yom Kippur. One long blast is sounded at the end of Yom Kippur. Learning to blow on the shofar is not difficult, but getting it to sound sweet and make the blasts that are the right length—whether short or long—takes some time.